# DISABLED

**Bandi Crawford**



ISBN 979-852-333-5167

Published by Bandi Crawford



www.bandicrawford.com

## Dedication

This book is dedicated to my eternally supportive family, to Christine 'Bitch' Beck who was the foundation for Tessa and the oh-so-weird but totally awesome bond the characters share, just as we do, and Charlotte 'Chaz' Rutter who inspired Tilly-Tok, continually defied disability boundaries and was the most glamorous yet down to earth farmer's daughter and gin connoisseur I ever met until her sad departing from this world.

## Acknowledgements

I'd like to thank my amazing friends (including care workers) for everything they do, particularly for tolerating the hours of urban exploring videos I make you suffer when I can't sleep!

I'd also like to say thank you to The Proper People (Bryan and Michael) and other urban explorers for all of the videos they put on YouTube who allow people like me to experience a corner of this beautiful and decaying world.

Additionally, I would like to thank Hindy Rahmatullah for the amazing cover, Gonzalo Mansilla for the fantastic page art and Tanbir Hasan for turning my sketches into beautiful floor plans.

I would like to thank Katelynn Koontz for her sensational editing, feedback and assistance, as well as Benjamin Steed for his beautiful copy editing and continuous support.

I would also like to thank Hugh Phoenix-Hulme for his wonderful formatting, solving all of my tech needs and especially for the remarkable level of support throughout this whole project. You have been a blessing!

And finally, to my icon and inspiration Keith Raniere to whom I will always be thankful.

And a huge thank you to the sponsors of this project: • Amber & Emily Roberts • Fallon Vendetta • Jan S • Hugh Phoenix-Hume • The Browns • Sonia Greaves • Sue H

Brandi Crawford

# TABLE OF CONTENTS

# DISABLED DECAY

Bandi Crawford

*"Extreme fear can neither fight nor fly"*
*— William Shakespeare*

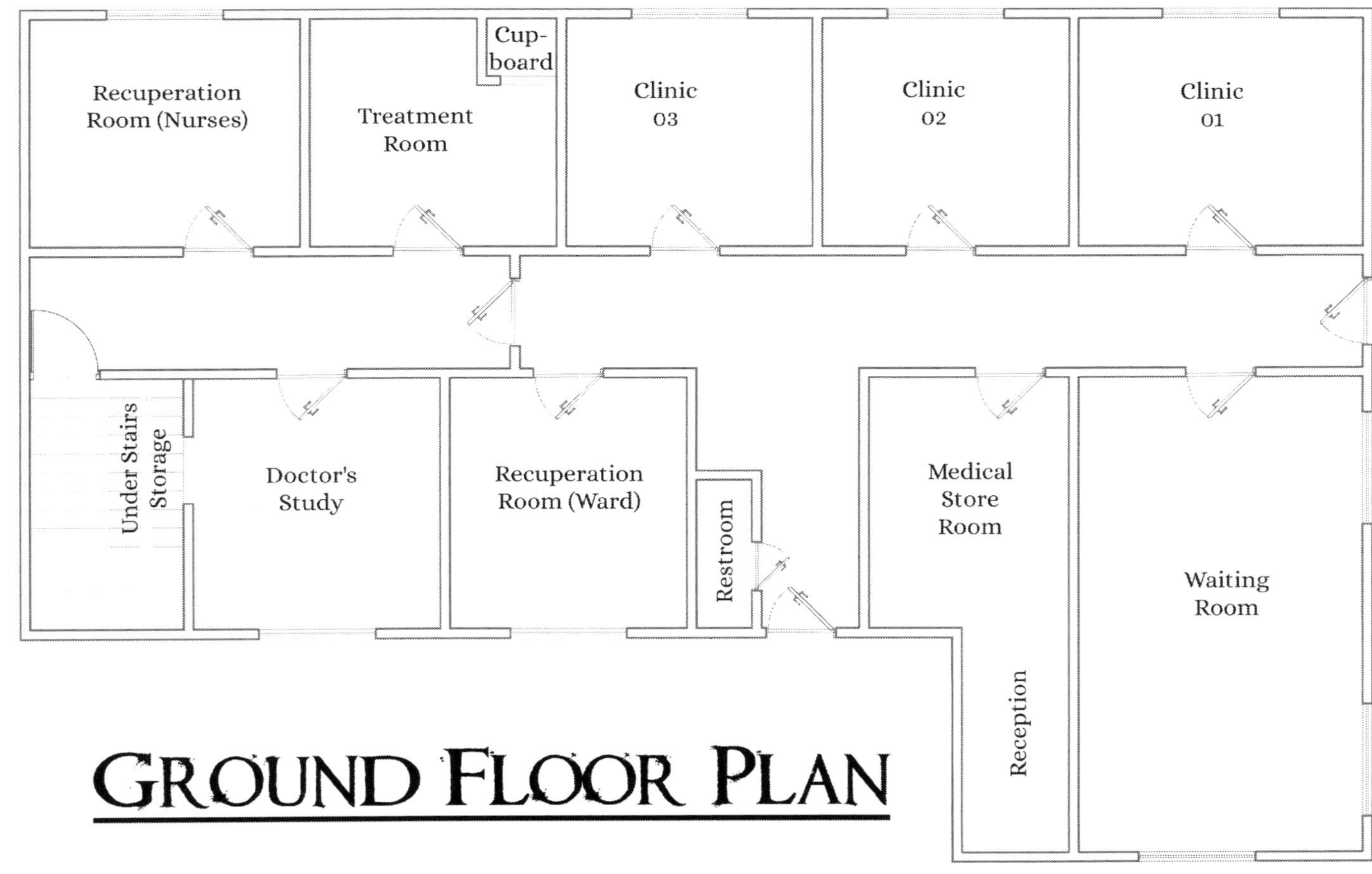


# Ground Floor Plan

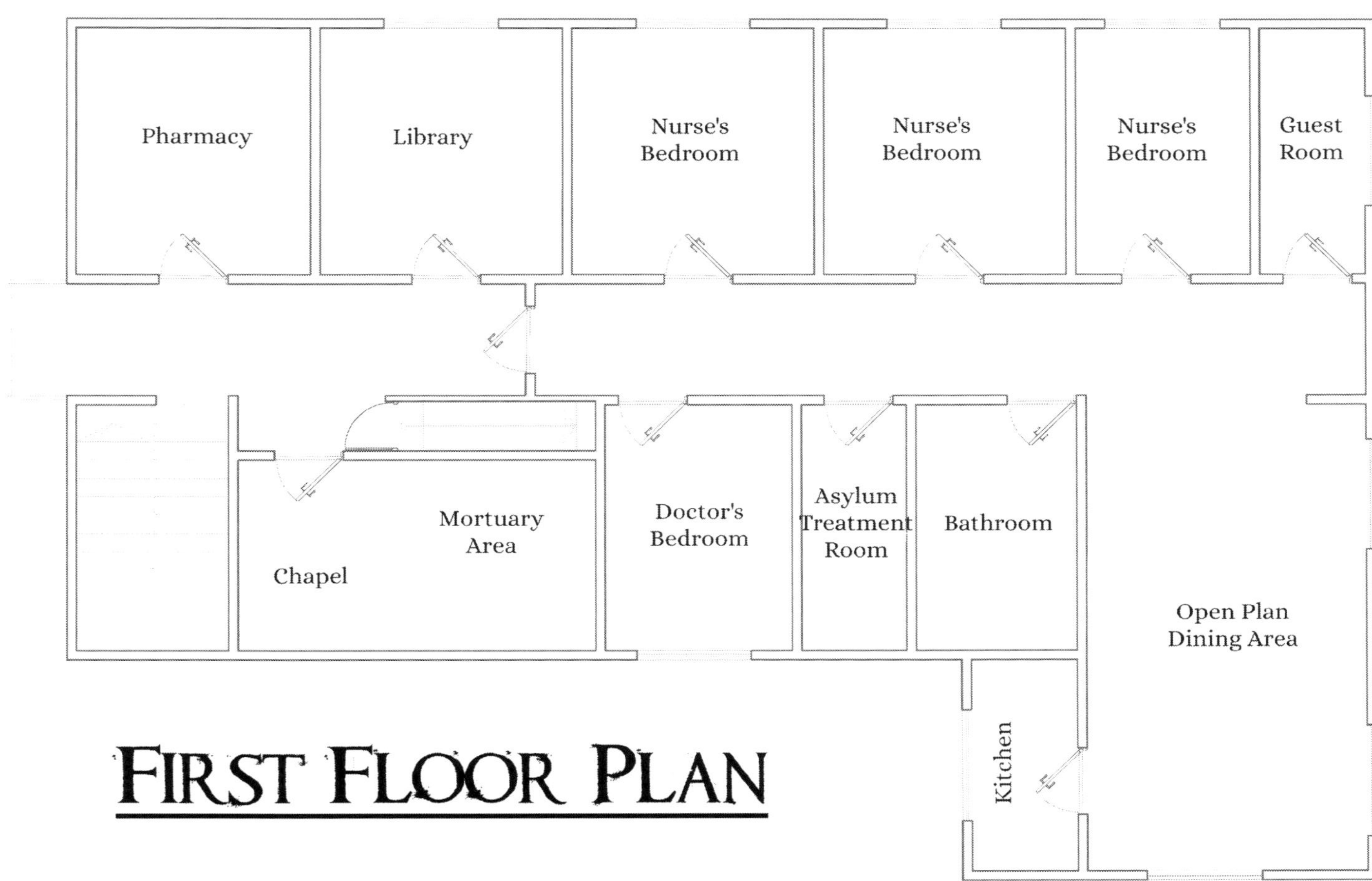
Pharmacy
Library
Nurse's Bedroom
Nurse's Bedroom
Nurse's Bedroom
Guest Room
Mortuary Area
Chapel
Doctor's Bedroom
Asylum Treatment Room
Bathroom
Open Plan Dining Area
Kitchen
FIRST FLOOR PLAN

# CHAPTER 1

The push wheelchair is easy enough to get along the dirt track and passing the barrier was only a matter of lifting up a bar. All that remains between the two women and the abandoned building is a padlock on a chain. Fortunately, they brought bolt cutters.

"This is totally against the rules of urban exploring," says the platinum blonde in the pinafore dress and wheelchair, even though there's a grin as wide as the summer sun on her face.

"We're not technically altering the place. We aren't damaging the building." Tessa flashes a smile. "So, really, are we breaking any rules?"

"Loads—but the rest of them I don't mind getting on camera. Just one snap should do it, and then we'll be in," says Tilly.

"Are you filming the front before we crack on?" The brunette clamps the cutters in the air briefly.

"You're learning."

The cutters are rested on the wall while Tessa gets the camera.

Turning her chair around so her back is to the building, the blonde runs a folded hand through her locks as her companion counts down the camera.

“Three . . . Two . . . One . . .” The red light blinks.

“Hi there, everyone. It’s me, Matilda Lock AKA your girl Tilly-Tok. As always on this channel, we’re proving that you can do everything I can do, and I can do everything anyone else can too. Today, I’ve brought my wheels and my high-heels to do a bit of urban exploring! We’re here at an abandoned location, as found by my partner-in-crime – even though she’s on the payroll – my support worker, Tessa.”

The camera swings around for a brief smile. “But it’s my day off, so no using this footage to report me for encouraging her!”

It pivots back.

“Though, it could be argued that by finding this place and helping me get in, *even* if it breaks a little red tape, it's doing your job well. Tessa likes to encourage independence, everyone. It’s why she got into care.”

“Because it sure as hell wasn’t to become a millionaire.”

They laugh. “It’s depressingly true. Anyway, for those of you who are new to the channel, I like to do things I’m told I can’t, and let you know that you can do them too! But why tell, when you can show? Urban exploring has always been a big dream of mine but places of the past

aren't exactly built with ramps and rails. Tessa found this gem when she was on the way to see family, and we're pleased to say it's accessible – or at least, *some* of it is. You never know what you're going to find in these kinds of places; fallen tiles, holes in the floor, flooding—"

"Ghosts."

Tilly-Tok rolls her eyes, tilting her double set of fake lashes upwards. "We watch way too many horror movies on night shifts . . . Anyway, if we see a ghost, you'll see it too – and hey! At least we wouldn't have to click bait a title."

There's a pause and a long "Umm . . ." before the blonde continues.

"Right! So, for those of you who don't know about urban exploring, it's basically embracing the past and looking around abandoned places. This one is an old doctor's surgery which was set up inside his home and has a ton of rooms. We aren't going to tell you the exact location because that breaks some of the unwritten rules of urban exploring. Because we don't want people coming in and trashing the place, the first rule of urban exploring is—"

"Don't talk about urban exploring?"

Tilly tilts her head, smirking. "This isn't Fight Club."

"First rule of Fight Club, don't talk about Fight Club."

"I don't even like that movie."

"You're kidding? It's a classic."

"The best part about it is Brad Pitt."

"More like Jared Leto."

"The Joker's in it?"

"The Suicide Squad Joker, he plays Angel Face."

The blonde raises her arms out. "I've only seen it once."

"So, you didn't even rewatch it after the—spoiler alert—flicker thing?"

"No."

"Next you'll be telling me you haven't seen A Clockwork Orange."

". . . Your taste in movies is messed up."

"You didn't like Clockwork Orange?"

"I mean . . . isn't it a bit twisted to say you 'like' something with that much . . . words I'll get demonetized for?"

"Breaking exclusive time; whether it's for the art or whatever, do you, or do you not, like watching A Clockwork Orange?"

"The book was pretty good."

The camera gets a lens-full of trodden grass. "You haven't watched A Clockwork Orange, have you?"

"It's on my to-watch list."

Tessa picks the camera up, aiming it at herself. "See, this is why she needs me, it's got nothing to do with her disabilities. She needs educating. Doesn't like Fight Club. Hasn't even watched A Clockwork Orange."

"Hey, I introduced you to Seven."

"Fair. That's a redeeming point, but you have a lot to learn."

Tilly puts her hands on her hips. "So do you, like the fact that every minute chatting about movies is a bit of sunlight we wasted."

"Time is never wasted when discussing the classics. You have a point, though."

"Camera up . . . Thanks. What we can tell you is that this place is going to be awesome. Let's go!"

Tessa turns the camera off and puts it in the bag on the back of the wheelchair, retrieving her cutters.

"Do you want to do it?" She holds out the massive bolt cutters.

Tilly shakes her head. "I don't think I can."

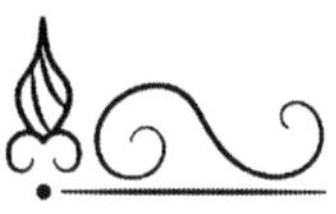

"I'm sure we could rig it somehow. We just need to think outside of the box. Fancy it?"

Tilly gnaws her lip and again shakes her head - this time with a camera quality smile. "With these nails? You've got to be kidding me."

"Your loss, this is going to be super satisfying."

Tessa clamps down with both hands firmly gripped around the handles, shaking as she squeezes. She has to hold off for a moment, flexing her fingers before going back in. This time she grits her teeth, palms turning pale against the mahogany of her skin with the amount of pressure she's putting on.

*Clank!*

She falls as it cuts, catching herself on her palms with a chuckle.

"Are you okay?" Tilly-Tok leans forwards. The wheelchair slips back on the mud. "Sh— sugar honey iced tea!" She grabs the wheels and pants through a wide smile.

"Better than you are. Did you just stop your heart or something?"

"Oh, shut up. Let's just get in there—and get some B roll." Tilly-Tok gets out her phone, which is much easier to hold than a clunky camera. It may not be a 1080p resolution, but it certainly gets the jobs done.

Tessa pulls the chain out with a rattle as it catches every link.

“Are you ready?”

The phone beeps. “Always.”

Tessa pushes at the door with baited breath. In fact, neither of them are breathing. If she can't get in this way, that’s the end of the adventure. Anywhere else she would climb into a window, throw her jacket over the broken glass and hope for the best, but here there are bars on them. If they can't get in through the door, there's no chance of her going in and moving anything that's in the way of the door.

Leaning into it, she groans. “It’s like it doesn’t want to open up, maybe if I just—ah-ha!”

The door creaks open, just enough to let out a whiff of mold.

“You got it!”

“A bit, I think it's stuck on something. Give me a second.”

Leaning all of her weight against it, the brunette heaves. At a glacial pace, the door slides open, gathering thick sludge in a curve.

“Just water damage. Sometimes it makes things swell. I hope it’s not too far in.”

Tessa squeezes through the narrow gap, taking the croppers with her. “Why? Scared to get your hands dirty?”

“Yes, actually. You try pushing one of these with your hands when it’s all goop like that.”

“For once, I don’t mind offering to push when you can do it yourself. This place reeks. Looks like it’s just built up though.”

Tessa drags the sludge out of the way with the cutters, making the door easier to open, and brings Tilly-Tok inside.

The air is thick with the dense smell of mold mingled with something chemical and pungent, almost disinfectant-like. Perhaps something of a bygone era, or maybe the fumes left over from old graffiti – although there’s not very much, which is surprisingly pleasant.

The facade of the building is like many others that the two women have seen online, with its crumbling exterior and rusting sign above the door. Inside is different; it’s about as well preserved as it could get given the amount of rainwater that has come in.

At the entrance, it has formed a black puddle of sludge that sits perfectly still, until her wheels put tracks in it that are instantly washed away as if they had never been there.

“Look at this place, it's so pristine.” Tilly says, airily.

“I think we have a different definition of that word. Jesus, it smells awful.”

Tilly-Tok's lips open just a shade. “For a place this old, it's pretty impressive. I was expecting more damage . . . Didn’t you say it was Victorian?”

“I’m only guessing by the building. I didn’t look anything up much,” Tessa admits. She takes a few exploratory steps around, testing the sturdiness of the floor.

“Huh,” Tilly hums. “I guess we’ll have to play detective to learn about this place, then.”

The downstairs isn’t particularly large. On the right-hand side of the corridor there are five doors, making the place about as big as the average town church. On the left is a battered waiting area – half subsided so that the chairs look as if they’re melting into the floor – followed by a few doors and then, at the end, a stairwell.

“What do you think is in there?” Tessa tries to peer through the grime-caked window at the side of the waiting area. With a series of splats, she moves to it.

“You are not going to touch that, are you?”

“You know, when you work in care, you have to deal with a lot of stuff. When I started at the old people’s home, before you,” she grunts, pressing her hand on the sliding frame and giving a push that does nothing.

"—they said that you aren't a real care worker until you've been through the unholy trinity."

Tilly leans forward. "The unholy trinity. What's that?"

"It's where you get peed on, pooped on and vommed on." She tries again but there's no movement.

"Did you complete it?"

"Many times over. It kind of doesn't register on your radar after a while."

"My radar doesn't need testing, thanks."

Tessa chuckles, wiping her hands on her jeans and dredging back. "It makes things like this no biggie. I'm glad you told me to wear old boots, though. Yeesh."

"I couldn't do what you do."

"As long as I can wash my hands later, we're good."

"I didn't mean . . ."

"Don't you be going all soft on me, I can deal with helping you shower but I am not okay with the fluffy stuff. You know that, besides, it's a bonus enough that I don't have to wipe your backside."

The blonde snorts. "But it's such a good looking one."

"You're not my type," Tessa chuckles.

"Anyway, how about we try that door?" Tilly says, glancing up the corridor.

"You could have told me that sooner!"

"You're the one who walked right into the puddle. Jeez, sometimes I'm sure I should be the one caring for you."

Tessa's coffee-painted lips pout, wrinkled up at the corners with a threatening smile. "You're doing a terrible job."

A draft rattles through the corridor and there's a bang.

"Hhh!" Tilly sky rockets so hard that the chair bounces. The main door has closed.

Naturally, Tessa starts howling. "You leaped so high you left the seat!"

"That was scary!" Her breaths are rapid as she places her hand on her chest. "I think my heart is in my throat."

With laughter and heart rate returning to a steady rhythm, they push the door open to the room with the sealed window. It's all files and folders, along with a couple of empty pill bottles on the side.

While Tessa flips through some of the ones which haven't turned to pulp with the water, Tilly films the room.

"This is next to the waiting area that we just saw, and it's full of paperwork. A lot of it is soaked but there's a lot

left. I read somewhere that it wasn't until the 90s or something that this kind of stuff had to be confidential. That's pretty freaky."

"Could look it up?"

"I'll add it in post, there's no data here. I barely have three bars of signal . . . What do you have there?"

Tessa signals to hand over the phone and scrolls it over the spread-out sheets. "Patient records, it looks like they were done on a printing press and then just scribbled on. Considering so many people couldn't read and write back then, some of these diagnoses have really long names." She taps on a page with writing so looped and swirling that it could easily be mistaken for a spider that rolled out of an ink jar. "Melancholia. That's depression I think."

Tilly glances around. There are shelves at the back with a few aged books. The pages look like they've been dipped in tea, but as she leans over and tugs one off the shelf, they sure don't smell like it.

"Let's look it up." She opens the cover with a creak and a weak flop as it pulls away from the poorly bound pages. "A low kind of delirium, with a fever; usually attended with fear, heaviness, and sorrow, without any apparent occasion – that's Beach's Family Physician."

"Delirium sounds like Alice In Wonderland."

"Yeah, like those 'Drink Me' bottles. I don't think I'd want to drink anything in here though."

Tessa says, “Dang, there goes my big stunt idea for the end of the video.”

“Me drinking old juice?”

“Bet you could get seriously drunk on juice this old.”

“More like I would have to go get my stomach pumped,” says Tilly, with a snort.

The sheets on the table rustle as Tilly flicks through the book. After a while she closes it and hums.

“What’s up?” Tessa puts down the set of papers that she had been looking through.

“Melancholia was usually treated in mental asylums, not doctors surgeries.”

“Weird.”

“It is,” says Tilly.

There’s a noise in the corridor and they both turn around, looking between each other and the open door. Everything becomes heightened; the sound of saliva gulping down their throats, the drip of a leak somewhere they haven’t yet seen and the movement in the corridor. It starts as a clicking, moving away from them. Something falls over – a box maybe? There’s quiet then.

Tilly lowers her voice so it’s barely a whisper. Still, it fills the room. “Do you think someone saw us come in?”

"Down that dirt track? Doubt it."

"Maybe it's another explorer?"

Tessa places the phone back on the blonde's lap and moves towards the door. She inches to it, peeking around.

"See anything?" Tilly questions, nervously.

The brunette steps into the corridor. "You're not going to believe this."

"What?"

"It's a crow." Tessa says, stepping back into the room. "Just a bird. Funny looking one, too."

Tilly-Tok releases a breath that had been holding in her chest far too long. "And here's me thinking we're going to bag some decent content!"

"Me getting murdered by a rando you mean? Come on." She pulls the chair towards her and Tilly puts the book on a shelf. "Let's find something mind-blowing, like an antique that's worth a million."

"You know we'd have to leave it? Be like a ghost, leave everything."

"Are you telling me you wouldn't take it home?"

"I mean . . ."

The two look around the ground floor while debating how much something would have to be worth to break

the code. A code, which Tessa tries to argue is “more of a guideline”. The treatment rooms have old benches and desks made of quality wood. Tilly has to wonder if there will even be places like this to explore in the future since everything is mass produced. The stuff here may be as old as Tilly-Tok’s joints often feel, but even over a hundred years on, there are remnants of lacquer on the table tops. The final two rooms are what seems to be a staff room with the added attraction of a game of snakes and ladders, and a store room crushed by a fallen tree.

“Now that I've thoroughly defeated Tessa at vintage board games, and it would have been cards too if they weren’t so wet, it’s about time to wrap up our mini-adventure. It’s been such a good time . . . Nope, this sign off isn’t right.” Tilly clicks, while Tessa sits on the bottom of the stairs filming her. The vlogger tries again, but the sign off doesn’t fit.

Tessa lowers her hands. “Do you want to try a different angle?”

“I’m not sure, it just doesn’t feel quite like we’re finished here.” Tilly isn't certain how to describe it. She’s just got a strange gnawing feeling in the pit of her stomach and it gets worse any time she thinks about leaving.

“Do you want me to run upstairs and get some B roll?” Tessa gestures at the staircase.

"You shouldn't go up there on your own. Being alone in old places isn't recommended."

Tessa swivels. "You could come up with me."

"I know you want to encourage independence and all that, but I think that's kind of out of my ability."

Tessa's gaze switches between the stairs and the wheelchair. After a few checks she stamps her foot down on the bottom step.

"It's solid wood. I could get you and the chair up there —if you don't mind a few bumps that is."

The inhale Tilly takes is like a child being told they can have anything in a toy shop. Despite it, she pulls her composure back.

"Wouldn't that be dangerous for your back?"

The brunette shrugs. "Bouncing a chair up some steps isn't hard, especially not after you've dealt with bed bound guys in their eighties who still eat as much as they did back in the day when they were working full-time in factories or whatever."

"I guess . . ."

"It's up to you." There's a twinkle in her eye. "But you did say it's not somewhere to explore alone."

Tilly doesn't need telling twice. Excitedly, she changes the plan and they set the camera up to bounce the chair

upstairs. As Tessa tilts it back, gripping the handles and pulling it up one step at a time, she makes sure to keep her footing tight.

“And by the way,” Tessa says between steps. “Just a reminder, this can’t be used as evidence against me . . . and one more . . . and we’re there!” She rolls the chair back another foot and kicks the break on, heading down to retrieve the camera, and quickly adding: “You better like and subscribe for that!”

“Wow . . .” The platinum vlogger gazes down the door-filled corridor.

“How are you feeling?” Tessa asks, walking back up.

Tilly-Tok turns her attention to the lens and winks. “High. Higher than I’ve been without an elevator in years, that is!”

“Good,” says Tessa. “I think that it’s about time we get moving. I’m seeing a lot of doors up here.”

“I wonder how many of them even open up? Like, do you think some of them are going to be locked?”

“I dunno, but there’s really only one way to find out.” Tessa moves to the door immediately opposite the stair landing. She tries the knob. “Not locked, just blocked!”

Tessa puts her shoulder into pushing. It still doesn’t budge right away.

While Tessa sets about trying to leverage the door open, Tilly can't help but look back down the stairs. She knows it's only the one flight, but everything seems so far away! This is exactly what she wants to prove to people in her videos. Anyone can do what they want. Sometimes, you just need to be creative in the solution.

There's a grunt, and then a creak of rusty hinges moving. "Got it," says Tessa. "And – it's just an old closet."

Tilly can't help but laugh. She undoes the brake and carefully wheels herself over to Tessa, careful to only use the inner wheels so she doesn't get a fistful of goop. It really is just a closet and an empty one, at that. "There's nothing in there."

There is, however, an unhealthy looking amount of sludge on the floor, and clinging to the walls. That must be what had the door stuck. It smells strongly of rotting wood.

"Nasty," says Tilly. "That was not worth the effort you put into opening it."

"And here I wanted some hundred year old bleach," laments Tessa. "Alright. There go my hopes and dreams. You pick the next door. Let's see if you have any more luck with this."

Tessa takes a moment to look down the hall. None of the rooms look particularly stand out. It's just doors, doors and more doors. She picks a door at random, pointing it out. "Second door on the left."

"Second door on the left it is," says Tessa, happily. She bounds to it and tries. "Not locked! And – not blocked, either! We're in luck, Tilly! Come on, let's check it out."

Tilly grins at their success. The gnawing pit is gone, replaced with pure excitement. This is going to be exactly the additional adventure that the vlog post needs!

# CHAPTER 2.

"Hopefully the footage came out well," says Tilly-Tok.

"There's another floor if not."

Tessa crouches at the side of the wheelchair and they watch the footage. The lighting is surprisingly good for the angle until part-way through.

"What was that?"

"What was what?"

"There was a shadow or something."

"Maybe it's the light hitting the bottom of the wheelchair?" She rewinds, playing again.

"No, it was behind you. Wait for it . . . in a second . . . there."

Tessa furrows her brow, rewinding again and squinting. At the top of the stairs, just behind her, there's a streak of a shadow – a slip of a thing, going from right to left. It's only on the screen for a handful of seconds, maybe even less than that.

"How the heck did you catch that?"

The blonde's lips twitch up at the edge. "Online, you have to observe every detail."

“Is that why you take pictures of every slice of cake you eat or cocktail you drink?”

“That’s just what the fans want.”

“Still weird.” They watch it back a couple more times, trying to pause it at the exact right spot to make the shape out. The only thing it catches is a stripe of translucent black. “Like this.”

Tilly looks around. “Maybe it was a shadow from that.” She points to a brass, gas light which hangs in the walkway. It swings softly as a chill cuts through a broken window. Nothing else on the second floor is moving.

“Kind of a weird angle, isn’t it?”

“That’s for the viewers to decide,” she says, panning her phone around. “Let’s see what treasures we can find on this floor.”

Tessa nods, pats the arm of the chair and stands up.

“What?” asks Tilly-Tok with a tilt of her head.

“Nothing. I’m going to put this away.” She returns the camera to the bag. “You’re better at getting the angles anyway.”

“Do you think the quality will be okay?” Tilly chews on her lower lip. She likes shooting the film with her phone, but there’s so little light in this building, she’s not sure that it will catch the odd details.

Tessa seems completely unconcerned by that. “Definitely. Where should we check first?”

They edge carefully around, filming upwards on occasion where a hole in the ceiling, filled only by beams, lets them view the upstairs. The ceiling panels, which were once exquisitely carved, are scattered about the hall. At one point in time, this building really had been lovely. Years and years of weathered disservice have left it a rotting, hulking beast.

Looking for something interesting, they start trying the doors. Every door on the floor is bolted shut or rusted over; all but one.

Tilly-Tok leans forwards to push it open, retracting her hand just before touching it. There are colored dots on the door like a paint splatter; rust, probably. She hesitates and sits back.

“Maybe just push it with the footplate.”

That works. The door is heavy and the hinges scream in protest. The sound sends a few bugs skittering out from their hiding places. Tilly makes a face.

“We’re going to need some serious showers when this is done,” says Tilly. “I hope that all the filth shows up in the shots. I mean, those bugs? Totally worse than anything else we’ve found so far.”

“I don’t know,” says Tessa. “I kind of like bugs.”

“You like moths. There’s a difference.”

In older times, doctors and nurses often had rooms at the surgery, yet the bed they find is far from a home comfort. There are no sheets or pillows, just a long slab of metal like a baking tray on top of a crank. Leather straps as thick as her fingers hang by the sides and there is a tray of objects that make the restraints necessary.

There is a metallic tang in Tilly’s mouth, and as she chokes it back, the particles meld together into a heavy ball which plummets into her stomach with a clang. There are forceps, spikes, small hammers like the ones that come in Christmas toffee selections, nails stained black and bronze, and syringes so wide that they could probably pick up paint.

“Look at those. This is messed up,” she murmurs, unable to take her eyes from the instruments.

“I didn’t think they did much surgery in these places.”

“Me either. I mean there was a time when they were convalescent homes after the war but . . . I guess they had to take some emergencies.”

Tessa picks up a bottle with a punctured top, tilting it from side to side. The yellowed liquid in the bottom has split like oil on water, and is held in more by the thick, sepia crust that has formed on it than the lid.

“Anaesthetic, I’d really want some of this if I were in here.”

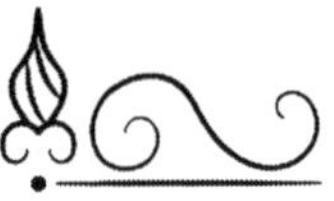

"Creepy to think I would have been in here, just because . . ." A shiver chases up Tilly-Tok's spine, weaving its way through each of her vertebrae. Just the thought is enough to make her nerves light up.

"On the plus side, you wouldn't fit much further in here," says Tessa. She edges around the tray and passes a row of cabinets, stepping behind a railed curtain. "That or they would have just manhandled you in."

"Tsh, I don't doubt it. Disabled, mental. Depressed, mental. Gay, mental. Abusive to men, mental. Foreign, mental. Abusive to your wife, justified. Times were broken." Tilly might like the aesthetic fashion choices from long ago, but everything else was abhorrent. No rehash of the Roaring Twenties for her, thanks.

There's a clank. "Speaking of broken, this window behind here is completely sealed shut."

"There's bars on all of them, I think. That's what it looked like from the outside."

Tessa borrows the phone to show Tilly the area after finding that the railed curtain is a little too unstable to move. The footage shows a series of wooden panels with nails hammered in. Between those and the window is a trapped curtain.

"You would think they would move the curtains first."

Tessa sits on the metal slab with a creak. "Unless they wanted it to look like the curtains were closed from the

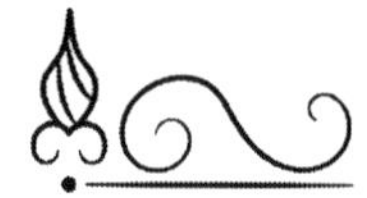

outside. It'd explain why the tiny room, too. They probably pretended it was a store cupboard or something to hide this." She draws back the fabric of the railed curtain a few inches and it starts to tatter in her hand, but not before Tilly gets a view of a high voltage contraption and what looks like two balls of cotton wool on the end of a headband.

"Electro-shock therapy. That's definitely not a regular doctor's domain . . ."

They sit in silence for a few seconds, the kind of moments that hang in the air like cobwebs. A slight swirl leaves Tessa's lips. There's something about being in this room that makes Tilly uneasy. It's not just the thought of how easily this could have been her fate – something about the way things are set up doesn't sit right with her.

Tessa must be feeling the same way. She hops down from her perch and reverses Tilly out of the door. "Let's get out of this one. It's freaking me out."

"I'm with you there," Tilly-Tok giggles. "This whole room is just . . . nasty. The viewers are going to eat it up, though."

"Well, that's always a plus." Tessa wiggles her way out of the room, and they start back down the hallway, heading towards the stairwell. "Do you think anyone's going to be able to figure out where this place is from that footage?"

“If they do, I hope they tell me in the comments.” Tilly snorts. “Okay, okay, that one wasn’t my best joke, I admit it. In all seriousness, I’ve got no clue. I guess it just depends on whether I have local viewers.”

Part way down the corridor, Tilly reaches down and hits the break. “Hold up.”

“Oof.” Tessa walks into the back of the chair with a chuckle. “You’re going to need to give me more notice than that!”

“Sorry.”

“No, you’re not.”

“True . . . Look up there again.” She points through the hole in the ceiling. With the sky outside beginning to tint with the first streaks of magenta, shadows are growing. One in particular had caught her eye. “You see that?”

“What is that?”

“It looks like there’s a bannister up there—”

“—which means there is a way up.” Tessa leans on the back of the chair with her arms crossed. Her fingers drum on the metal. “It makes me wonder, with a room like that, what else are they hiding?”

“Right? I didn’t see a staircase though. No drop ladder hatch either.”

Tessa moves away, running a hand over the walls. She knocks here and there with the back of her knuckles, freeing a cascade of dust and making her cough. She wafts a hand in front of her face.

"Be careful, there might be asbestos."

Tessa coughs again. "Or there might be an entrance." Brushing its way through the dust cloud is a thin strip of light, lining up with the edge of one discreetly placed panel. She hooks her fingers underneath, pulling it a little wider, but the weight is too much.

Tilly asks, "wait, where are you going?"

Tessa promises, "don't worry, I'll be right back. I'm just going to grab something to help open the hatch with."

"We shouldn't split up."

"It will take me thirty seconds. Promise," says Tessa. Walking back to the surgical room, she fetches the forceps. When she gets back, she says, "see? I told you, it wasn't going to take me any time at all."

Tilly rolls her eyes. "Just be careful getting it open. I don't want this trip to end with you bleeding."

"Don't worry about it, I'll be careful," says Tessa. She closes them, and then wedges them inside the crack and says, "never accuse me of doing things the way they were intended," as she hauls open the devices – and with them, the door.

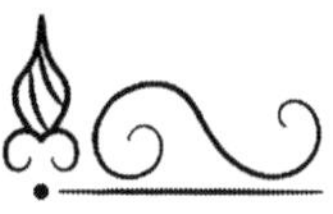

“No way!” Tilly beams. “I can’t believe that actually worked! Talk about having a big MacGyver moment.”

“We might find our millions yet!”

“We’re still not taking anything.”

“Especially not if there’s a dead body up there . . . That could earn you millions though. Can you imagine what your viewers would think?”

Tilly taps her forehead. “We’re not taking anything out of here . . . and we’re not Logan Paul!”

Placing her foot on the bottom step, Tessa turns back with a grin. “You say that, but we all know what you think of Logan Paul!”

Tilly narrows her eyes as her cheeks fill with crimson. “Get up there and see if there’s a way I can get up.”

“Taking control, I kind of like it . . . Is that how you’d talk to Logan?”

“Oh my God! Get out of here!”

“What? I can go on my own now? Aren’t you worried about me? Changed your mind on that one quick enough. I see how it is.”

Tilly smirks. “Mind you don’t fall through a rotten step on your way up.”

"Bitch," Tessa chuckles. "Seriously though, are you going to be alright on your own while I check it out?"

"Yeah. No worries. I promise not to go running off anywhere."

"And you've got your phone?"

"When do I not have my phone?" And then Tilly adds, "you're the one climbing up the mystery stairs. I'm pretty sure that I should be asking you these questions, not the other way around."

"Good point. Alright, I'll catch you in a minute." Tessa sinks into the darkness, but not without calling back: "And no sliding into Logan's DMs while I'm gone like a stalker."

"Shut up, Tessa!" Tilly's whole face feels red. She's certain to be blushing something awful.

"I got your back," Tessa calls over her shoulder. She vanishes from sight, chuckling.

As the laughter trails away with muffled footsteps, Tilly-Tok is glad to be out of that particular conversation. Except . . . The silence starts to sink in. It's all consuming in its nothingness. The last scraping footstep vanishes, and then there is just the sound of Tilly's own breathing, suddenly amplified by the sheer emptiness of the room.

Dust motes are still swirling gently through the air at the base of the hidden stairs. Tilly tries to focus on them

for the moment, but her attention keeps slipping. Her fingers curl tightly around her phone. For a moment, she's tempted to call Tessa and speak with her the entire time she's up there but – no.

Tilly isn't going to do that. She has to force herself to loosen her grip, trying to instruct herself through breathing normally. It's hard. She's already hyper aware of how the air is filling her lungs, the tightness in her chest on each exhale, the tang of dust with each inhale. It's never more difficult to breathe than when you're trying to do it 'normally'.

A year or two ago she wouldn't have been able to do this; not just the exploring - finding this doctor's surgery was a huge stroke of luck - but sitting alone.

She's never been bullied, no more than the typical school yard name calling anyway, and she has a great family. Growing up disabled though, with a condition that slowly deteriorates; it's . . . well, she has many friends, but long silences with room to think past the moment aren't one of them. Life is fragile, for some more than others. It makes the idea of another thirty years seem like it might go in a flash.

She shakes her head, dispelling the thought and gazing around. There has to be something down here that she can focus on, instead of just her own thoughts! Tilly doesn't want to play on her phone and risk running the battery down. If she just keeps sitting here in silence, it's going to make her scream.

She doesn't need to be worried, though, because a sound draws her gaze. First, the teeth-grating slide of metal and then the groan of a door. Both are from a room behind her, and when she looks back, one of the locked doors is open.

"Tessa. Tessa?"

Silence.

She tries again, "Tessa? Did you find another way down?"

Still, nothing.

Tilly heaves a sigh. "I hope that's that bloody crow . . ."

# CHAPTER 3.

With her mouth turning as dry as burned toast Tilly heads towards the door. It occurs to her that perhaps she ought to have packed a diazepam or two. Admittedly, she hasn't needed one for a while and they are supposed to be for her muscles over anything else; they do come in handy for anxiety, though.

And oh, but her anxiety has just turned itself into a spike jammed through her heart. It sits as a weight in her throat, and a strange tightness in her chest. Still trying to remind herself to breathe, she picks her way, slowly, down the hall.

"Calm down," she tells herself as the spokes turn in a stop-start motion, rolling on one push at a time. "She's probably pulling pranks . . . Like the time she flicked the lights off during Silent Hill. It's just Tessa being dumb."

That, or the crow from before managed to figure out how to open up locked doors. Tilly would happily accept either explanation at this point.

Going back past the room with the surgery table in, Tilly winces, feeling another chill; this time colder and thicker like blended ice trickling through her bones. Her hands pick up the pace as she clears the door, certain there was something inside . . . But that can't be, can it? With a flick of her long lashes, she glances again. Nothing.

The room is empty. The hall is still and quiet. Tilly appears to be the only one on this floor. As she nears the door, she gives her friend one last chance to end the prank early and come out, calling, “Tessa, I know it’s you. This isn’t funny. Just tell me what you found upstairs and let’s move on with things.”

But there’s no answer. Either Tessa is really sticking to her joke . . . or she’s not found a secret way down after all.

Tilly reaches the door and pushes it with her chair. The hinges continue to complain. It causes a rush of air that stirs up even more dust, sending Tilly into a sneezing fit as she tries desperately to wave it out of her face.

There have been some pretty amazing things found in abandoned places, like Rosie the Shark which was the video that started Tilly's binge into the world of urban decay; that being buildings that have been left to rot where they stand, like graves left open, to decay on their own time or stay forever as a skeletal reminder of the past.

People have found some amazing things on these trips. Tilly’s watched a lot of videos on the matter, done her research, knows the rules. Finding a formaldehyde soaked great white is probably a bit of a stretch out here, though.

But it seems she’s hit the jackpot. There might not be any sharks, but the room itself is filled with other marvellous treasures.

“Look at this!” Tilly is leaning into the room before the base of her seat has cleared the door frame. The old pharmacy is stacked to the brim with old bottles and jars. Their peeling labels are still easy to read and the selection of colors, although she doesn’t fancy trying any of these remedies, are as gorgeous as autumn leaves. There are browns like bark, orange syrups as thick as sap, things which look like liquid amber and crystallized honeys. Bandages are still rolled up in a box that has grown as brittle as a fortune cookie's shell. There’s no doubt in her mind; this will go viral.

People love this sort of thing. The fact that so many of the bottles are still intact just adds to its charm and rarity.

She raises her phone to film, creasing her brow at the way the battery has just about dropped to half, and lets it sway along the shelves. The Mahnomen Drug Co. sits in front with a corked bottle, some of which has crumbled into the bottle itself, followed by the diagonal sweep of Peacock’s Bromides' lettering. Little, brown bottles are lined up with ingredients like alphozone, salol and saltpeter. There’s not a paracetamol in sight, just row after row of autumnal glass, occasionally punctuated with forget-me-knot blue refills.

Which of these would she have been given? She can’t help but wonder about it. People were treated so differently back then. Tilly could have been forced to undergo any sort of treatment, whether she wanted it or not.

Her throat is starting to feel tight again. She scolds herself, “stop thinking like that!”

Under the well-stocked shelves is a double cupboard, slightly open. The edge is grimy so she uses her torch setting to get a look inside. There are a couple of big bottles and a box of syringes; definitely not worth touching.

Unlike the surgery room, the floor in the pharmacy is fairly clear, and she’s able to maneuver her chair around the shelves with relative ease. Dirt and grime crunches beneath the wheels of her chair. On the far end of the room, it looks like something – a rat, probably – has broken a few of the bottles at some point. The orange and brown glass glitters in the fading sunlight, the tile around the mess tacky with honey colored tincture.

Moving further into the room, Tilly finds that the window up here is quite clear, aside from the corners which are crammed with cobwebs. Just like the windows downstairs, this one has thick iron bars on the outside of it.

“Weird.” Tilly reaches up, using the back of her hand to wipe away the settled dust.

Outside the sun has dropped below the trees but the garden, which is more of a field with sparse trees, is still clear. The grounds are a decent size, by modern standards anyway. Tilly's own doctor’s surgery has a patch of grass that she could barely fit on, next to a car

park that is never more than half full. Places like this though, they roll on forever.

It's part of the appeal for the shoot. This is going to make great B-roll, too. She sets her camera up and starts trying to catch some footage of the setting sun and the impending twilight hour.

Tilly spots a flash of ivory out in the grounds and her phone slips from her grip and rattles on the floor, camera turning off.

"Sugar." She glances at it, and back at the window. Her eyes pulled into perspective with a squint, narrowing in on what appears to be someone dressed as an old-time nurse. Tilly curses herself as she looks at the person in period wear. Of course, there are going to be other kinds of explorers here. Sometimes people come for photo shoots; cosplayers and models trying to add some edge to their portfolio. Tilly-Tok should know; she's snapped a few shots herself.

As the woman reaches about a hundred meters away, it's easy to pick out some of the details of her attire. The costume in question isn't the kind Tilly would go for. If she was modelling, she supposes that she would like something cuter and more fitted. This one has impractical, puff-ball shoulders and a sort of apron dress. The hat is cute, though, she'll give her that. And maybe this lady is going for the historical society. Who knows? Regardless, it would be remiss of Tilly to miss the shot.

She can always grab her permission when they cross over since the nurse is definitely heading her way.

The blonde bends to pick up her phone, thankful that it wasn't the downstairs ooze it fell in. Had it fallen there, the bog could keep it! Straining, she hooks the corner with her folded fingers, dragging it towards her. She sits up for a half second to catch a breath before leaning down again. Even slender as she is, pressing double against her legs is a pain. Limited movement is one thing, creasing yourself in two is another. Screw the disabilities, this kind of yoga is hard! Pinching the phone between the heels of her palms, she hooks the device up.

"Gotcha!" She puffs, putting it on her lap to swipe the camera up. The screen lights up, though it seems like her signal has taken a battering. One bar is enough to call if she needs to, or maybe do a quick live stream if her battery allows. As for filming, neither matters.

She flicks it up between the window bars, switching between screen and scenery.

"Where did she go?" Tilly frowns. She cranes forward, trying to see if the woman has just stepped behind the ancient, dried up fountain, but no.

There's nobody on the grounds now. Not even a stray cat.

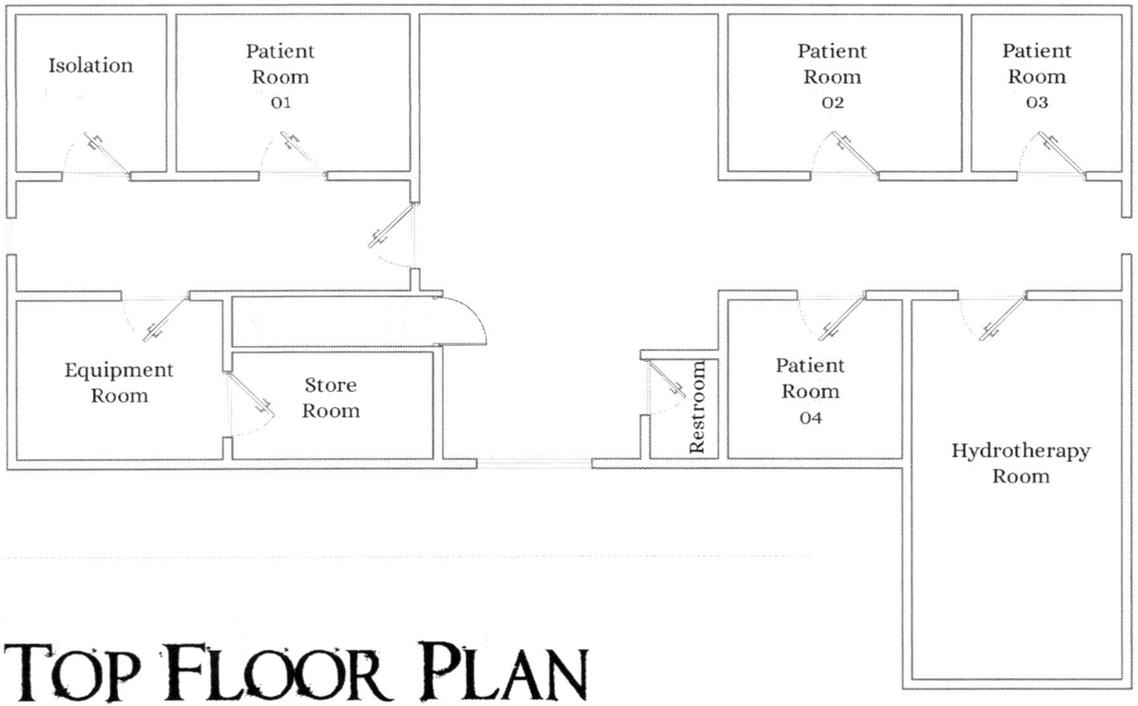

Isolation

Patient Room 01

Patient Room 02

Patient Room 03

Equipment Room

Store Room

Restroom

Patient Room 04

Hydrotherapy Room

# TOP FLOOR PLAN

# CHAPTER 4.

Tessa reaches the top of the stairs, met with a view of yet another corridor. This one, however, is shorter and at the end there is a pitched window that exits onto a little balcony; though, there's not much in the way of anything left of it with the overgrown trees ambushing it. It's hard to tell where one lot of wood ends and another begins. The sill is equally dogged; no chance of perching on that to take in the views, which is a shame since there are several birds flitting about outside. They sing the dawn chorus punctually, offering their melodies to the skies to anyone who wishes to share their company over the next hour or so.

Anywhere else, Tessa would have loved to sit around, but the doctor's surgery is too dangerous to be tiptoeing around at night. Despite that, it's nice to see a bird in this place that doesn't look like it wants to audition for an Alfred Hitchcock movie.

Pulling away, Tessa is mindful of her footing. That ominous hole in the floor is only a few meters away, and what they had thought was a bannister was really a handrail outside of a room with a tiled floor.

"This place just gets weirder," she says, standing on tiptoes as if that will help her see any more of the frosted blue and beige tiles. If there's a bathroom, the cave-in was

more than likely caused by water, she reasons, stepping to the nearest door. It's no wonder that there's such an awful smell clinging to the air.

"It should be safe enough in these couple of rooms." Tessa opens the first door, and it's surprisingly easy. There are four beds, all with rotted mattresses and one with a rag doll that is decidedly more 'rag' than 'doll'. Even if there was a way to get Tilly up here through this room, she's seen *Annabelle* – it's not happening. She shudders, imagining the doll looming near her as she brought Tilly up the stairs. Just for good measure, she closes the door on it, torn between wondering if she really has just seen too many movies and hoping that the door stays shut.

The next room is more promising. An old wheelchair sits slap bang in the middle; a funny looking thing. It's made of dark wood and has larger wheels at the front than at the back – an asset for not driving like a shopping trolley, no doubt. The footplate is little more than a flap and the seat has a moth-eaten cushion on it which rekindles unpleasant memories of TV dinner trays with lumpy, bean filled bottoms. The cushion isn't attached and she pulls it off by one corner, letting it slump in a sad pile on the floor.

She taps on the seat; not the most luxurious thing she's ever seen, yet certainly not the worst, especially if some of the equipment in the store cupboards at the old people's home are added into the equation. If Tilly didn't mind sitting in it for a few minutes, Tessa could fold the

modern wheelchair up and carry it through the corridor without a problem. They just might have to neglect the fact that it'd mean carrying the girl upstairs. Deleted footage doesn't count.

Tilly-Tok is barely seven stone, and Tessa has lifted her before, not that the powers that be would approve if they knew. But they don't, and the blonde is way easier to get around than her friends on a night out. On more than one occasion she's had to prop up Maisey, Carter and Greg after too much to drink and a bucket of fried chicken to top it off. It's just what people do.

Tessa brushes the dust off the back of the chair with her hand, instantly wishing she hadn't. The smears it leaves on her jeans as she drags it off are more dirt that distressed the denim. She planks down on the seat, leaning back and resting her arms on the side.

"Sturdy enough," she says.

A breeze catches her cheek, sending a silky strand of hair over it. She reaches up, tucking it back and shifting her gaze behind her. There's a crack in the glass, but it's one which doesn't appear to go all of the way through.

Tessa is about to get up when a faint buzz catches her attention. Her ears twitch up, angling the canals to the sound. It seems to be coming from the other end of the corridor. What it is, however, is unclear. When she tilts her head to the left it could be a sweeping brush, to the

right it's almost a distanced shout when under the waterline of a hot bath.

She stands, shifting out of the door. There it's more of a muffled sound, mixed with a crackle. She edges up the way until the floor arches under her boot. The hole is just ahead, and Tilly isn't in sight.

Odd words float her way. ". . . last . . . walk . . . –ment . . . search. Value to . . . our work."

Quiet drops over the place for a while before being dispersed by birdsong. The chilled breeze is gone, but Tessa still can't help feeling unsettled. "Too many horror movies," she mutters to herself. "You're letting things go to your head."

She rocks her head, making her way back to the corridor. Just as she'd thought when looking down the stairs, there's no sign of Tilly. The hallway is empty. Still. The silence from upstairs seems to be clinging to her shoulders and for a solid five seconds, Tessa isn't sure if she should break it.

Then her concern for Tilly over rides her fear and she calls out, "Tilly? Where are you at? You better not be playing nurse in that treatment room."

"No, down the end. I found a wicked pharmacy." Tilly doesn't sound hurt, which is an upside. She actually sounds pretty excited.

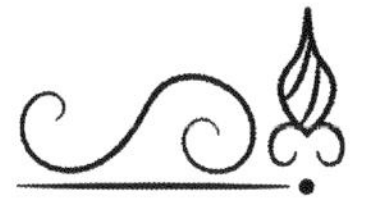

Tessa scampers down the way. “Nice! How the heck did you get in here?”

She shrugs. “The door opened. I think the wind blew it open. At least, I hope that’s what did it.”

“Bet it’s haunted.” Tessa says it without thinking, her mind drifting to the spooky dolls she had found upstairs.

Tilly’s cheeks drain of color, leaving her flesh marvelled with white. “You didn’t feel a draft?”

“Briefly, it must have been a pretty big gust. It came through the tiniest gap upstairs.”

“Did you find a way up?” Her color cascades back in.

“Yes, and no.”

“That’s helpful,” the blonde scoffs with a smirk.

“There is a way up, but you’ll have to get out of your chair.” Tessa gestures over her shoulders, towards the door leading back into the hall.

“You do realize I’m not in this thing for kicks, right?”

“And here I was thinking you were faking it just so you could employ my awesome self,” Tessa replies. “I can carry you up there, there’s an old wheelchair in one of the rooms.”

Tilly-Tok runs a hand through her hair. “Is that safe?”

“I’ve carried you before.”

Her hand pauses. “I mean the chair.”

“I sat in it okay.”

“Huh,” she hums, bringing her hand down and tucking her phone in the pocket on her pinafore dress. “And it’s fairly clean?”

“Yes,” Tessa gives a theatrical curtsy. “Your majesty. Oh, pristine princess!”

She raises her hands in submission. “Hey, I’m game if you are.”

Tessa straightens up. “We need to go on more adventures. It’s bringing you right out of your shell.”

“Anything for the views . . . That reminds me; we need to be quick about this if we’re going to get the first scoop. There’s someone else here.”

“Did they have a uniform?”

“Nope, awesome outfit though. I think they’re another explorer or cosplayer or something.”

“Informative,” Tessa teases. “Why were you by the window anyway?”

“For footage. Speaking of, we’re going to need some of the high-up ones. Can you get them on the camera, please? My battery is shot.”

Tessa retrieves the camera, taking the opportunity to swipe another baby wipe on her hands as she goes in the bag. "That's weird. Your plug might be dying. It looks like this is losing charge fast too."

"Freaky. Let's hope the toaster hasn't blown up when we get back."

"Not with how little juice it's putting out." She films the top few shelves which are out of reach and turns the rapidly failing camera off. "Speaking of freaky, were you on your phone earlier?"

"You're going to have to be more specific than that."

"When I was upstairs."

"Oh, yeah, but I dropped it. I ended up having to reach down and grab it. Maybe that's what rattled the charge."

"Maybe. There's not much to see up there so it should last." She takes hold of the wheelchair and they roll towards the secret stairwell.

"Anything on the level of the lost lab they found in London with all that crazy taxidermy?"

"Thankfully no, but there is a creepy doll up there."

Tilly grins. "I feel like I'm going to need a close up of that."

"Then you can take it yourself!"

Laughter bursts into the air. “You sure?”

“Very!” Tessa says, firmly. No way is she going near that doll again. Just knowing it’s up there is bad enough. “If the door to the doll room is open when we get there, I’m leaving.”

Tilly asks, “you closed it?”

“Of course I closed it,” says Tessa, indignantly. “I don’t want it running around while we’re here!”

“You know, there was once this group of people who found a sealed box floating towards them and when they opened it there was a random doll in it looking right back at them.”

“There better not be anything like that up here or you’re on your own.”

“What about your duty of care?” She pokes her tongue out.

The brunette stops the chair, checking that the steps are still clear. “You know in care homes, the policy if there’s a fire is to high tail it out and let the fire brigade deal with the residents.”

“That’s brutal.”

“It’s another reason I couldn’t stick it there, even though I miss the residents.”

“You don’t visit?”

“You’re not supposed to.”

Tilly laughs. “So, when are you next visiting?”

“Tuesday. I’m not missing out on Doreen's birthday. Somebody has to take her the caramels she likes. And I promised Doris and Molly a game of Go Fish.”

“I knew it. You’re such a softie.”

“Ehh . . . It’s a dumb rule anyway. Are you ready?”

A long breath leaves Tilly-Tok’s lips. “As I’ll ever be.”

“For the views.”

She nods. “For the views.”

# CHAPTER 5.

Leaning down to the chair, the two work together. As Tessa leans to put Tilly over her shoulders, Tilly shifts her weight onto her.

“I think this is what they call a fireman's lift.”

“More like something from Magic Mike,” replies Tessa as she stands. “Watch your head. I would not want to knock you out.”

“Really? Shocking.” The blonde laughs.

“You do pay my wages,” Tessa gives back.

Tilly sniggers, though it’s a little compressed as Tessa begins to take her up the stairs. “Knocked out is better than getting dirt in my hair.”

“Are all vloggers this vain?”

“Just the good ones. What the—” Tilly’s body tenses.

Glancing up, Tessa keeps walking. There’s nothing catching. “What’s up?”

“I saw that nurse cosplayer girl again. There were a few of them.”

“I’ll check it out when I go back to get the chair.”

Tilly-Tok hesitates. "Alright."

Her inhale is so sharp that Tessa can feel it pressing against her shoulder as they reach the upper steps. She has to admit, with looking for a way to get Tilly up, she had hardly taken in the details of the hidden floor.

It's smaller than Tessa had originally thought; there are only four doors on the right and three of them on the left. The door to the room with the doll in it is, thankfully, still closed. Tessa only feels a little silly to realize she's actually very relieved to see it. She can handle all of the slime, grime and dust that this place has to throw at her, but that doll was absolutely pushing her limits.

There's a single light hanging from the ceiling, the sort that's built to work off of a pull string. The string is long gone, however, and the light sways ever so slowly on the breeze. The cool air is drifting in from between the cracks of the walls which are holding up surprisingly well. Then again, they do look much heavier duty than the ones downstairs. The hole in the floor is about halfway down. A mass of cobwebs crosses a good portion of the upper gap, the thick webbing long since blotted over with dust.

Tessa angles her body towards it. "That's where we originally saw this place from. Can you believe we almost left without even knowing this was up here? That just seems wild to me."

Tilly nods. "This place has to be hidden in the roof or something. It doesn't look like there are three floors from outside."

Tessa's steps seem unnaturally loud in all this quiet. She hurries to where she left the old-fashioned wheelchair sitting. "No windows that I could see outside. I guess they must be the slanted kind."

"Just spooky dolls?" Tilly grins and then, "oh wow, that chair is old."

"It's sturdy," reminds Tessa. "I checked."

Placing Tilly onto the chair, Tessa rolls out her shoulder with her fingers edging into the crease.

"Am I that heavy?"

"Hardly. I'll go grab the chair and check out who is hanging out down there." She clicks her fingers before heading off, adding: "Then we'll get a picture of you in that. Perfect thumbnail."

Trekking quickly down the stairs, Tessa's boots thunder. She hops the last two in one—and halts.

The wheelchair is rolling down the corridor, gliding away from her. Tipping her head to the side, Tessa watches it. It passes one doorway, then two and stops. For a short time, she pauses.

When she takes her next step, her footprint is barely left behind when there's a scraping metal sound at the

end of the corridor. A door at the end opens. The sound comes again—closer.

Her foot flattens on the ground, backing up.

The next door is opening.

There it is again. A bolt lifting, a locked door opening.

Closer and closer.

The air grows frosty, so cold that her lungs begin to ache. A blast hits her like a sharp slap in the face.

"Tilly!" she gasps, turning to run up the stairs as the last door opens.

She bolts up the stairs, pulse pounding wildly in her veins. All she can think about is getting to Tilly before something bad happens. She risks a glance over her shoulder, but can't see anything. Her foot doesn't clear the next step completely and she lurches, scrambling. Her palms hit the wood of a higher step, hard enough that they scuff. She all but launches herself back onto her feet and keeps going.

Though she didn't outright see anything working the doors, Tessa knows innately that something has just gone terribly wrong, and there is no way it was by a human hand. It's the sort of gut-shrinking realization that hits you in the dead of night when you hear a noise just outside of your bedroom window; a natural fear response that sends her scrambling back towards her charge.

As she reaches the top of the steps, she skids to a halt. A nurse stands in front of her, bedecked in the garb of an 1800s health worker. The cap on her head is similar to a nun's habit, but there's nothing holy about the pale glass of her eyes.

Before Tessa can scream, there's a sharp pain in the side of her neck.

"Kkh!" Tessa spews the sound, immediately feeling her body beginning to slump. Her blurred gaze follows the pain and it leads her to an enormous glass needle lodged in the side of her neck. The plunger is fully sunken in by a hand as pale as the tight cuffs on the wrists of its owner.

Whatever was inside it is now deployed into her body.

Everything goes fuzzy, swaying as if the doctor's surgery has sunk into the sea. She can't pick out one thought from the next; they just bleed together, fluid and loose. Her limbs tingle. It starts in her fingers and rapidly climbs upwards, taking a life of its own and bleeding into her the way ink does into water. Tessa makes an attempt at swatting the nurse's hand away, but she misses by a mile. Her hand flops.

The nurse pulls the needle and syringe back. Tessa staggers sideways, her shoulder hitting the wall. There's a part of her that's concerned about going down the stairs backwards, but it's distant and far away. She thinks about Tilly, but that thought is just as hard to hold onto.

"Wh'di'ou . . ." It's the best that Tessa can get out. Her tongue won't cooperate. Her vision turns to milk. She makes another attempt at grabbing for the nurse, but her arms barely flop around. Her legs shake, tremble and then give out completely.

Tessa hits the floor and her eyes flutter shut. The steady clop of kitten heels moves along the corridor as something clamps her ankles. The floor is moving underneath her as something drags her along like a tired child dragging a raggedy, old teddy bear by a limb.

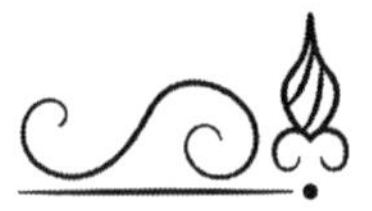

# CHAPTER 6.

Sitting in a new wheelchair is always a bit weird, kind of in the same way new shoes need to be worn in. All of the components are there; they just aren't quite right. Tilly-Tok wiggles her bottom and leans forwards a little. She's not adverse to sitting on hard surfaces and she quite enjoys the rope swing she, Tessa and Jodie made in the summer even though it's a plank and some ropes. Her discomfort is a small price to pay for views and freedom, and in this case it's more of a dull ache anyway; one she can manage by shifting her weight. It occurs to her that this wheelchair in particular is more like new shoes than others, since it's bearable yet getting out will be the same satisfaction as tugging off boots at the end of the day. If it is a shoe, it's not an attractive one. Though it does have the same effect as those awful tan slippers old people wear once they no longer care for style over comfort.

She checks her phone; 32% battery and no signal, but enough to get a quick video. She aims it at herself first.

"So, we made it up to the roof area. Don't ask us how, we're entitled to have as many secrets as this place seems to! Judging by the carpet of dust up here, it looks like we were the first to be up here in, well, years. Crazy, right? Check this out." She puts the phone on her lap to turn it over and raises it up again to capture the scene in front of her. The window is so sunken that there's little chance of

seeing in from the outside, perhaps a slither of light if there had been one. There's nothing on the ceiling and no sign of a handheld or candle anywhere. Outside, years of fallen leaves and rainwater have settled into a pulp on the glass, and a good three inches above it is stained bottle green. These windows too, have bars. They're screwed so tightly into the inside walls that the plaster seems to have cracked years before it was ever abandoned. Tilly draws in a long breath and pans around, catching nothing in particular beyond peeling paint and clusters of dead flies in the corner.

She finds herself coming back to the window, hovering for a long moment as she speaks.

"Do you see those cracks up there? It makes me wonder how deep they drilled it, and how—actually . . . I'm pretty sure the Victorians didn't have power tools . . . They were big on industry, though. There's the industrial revolution and all that." Her arms start to weigh heavy. "Or maybe somebody tried to rip it off and get away. That's a scary thought . . . What do you think happened? Why is this place even here? What was it for? Let me know in the comments section and I'll try to find some clues for the end of the video." Tilly-Tok strains her arms to keep the phone up for a lingering look.

After five seconds of holding her breath, she turns the footage off and slips the phone away again.

Craning her head back, Tilly's perfectly contoured brow creases.

"Tessa? Tess."

Silence.

The blonde looks at the large wheels which are set on the front of the chair. Sure, they're easier to reach there but there is no way her bare hands are going on those tetanus-coated disks.

Her nostrils narrow, pulse picking up in her ears as the lobes tingle with warmth.

"Are you alright, Tess?" The beating picks up traction, only dropping again when there is the clip-clop of steps coming down the corridor after some sort of scuffle. Tilly-Tok places her hand on her chest.

The modern metal comes into view and she straightens up.

"You totally tripped on the top step, didn't you? I can't take you anywhere." Tilly laughs.

Suddenly, there's a gripping of her waist and she's hooked backwards. The air is forced from her as she lets out a frightfully unattractive sound. Her hair falls over her face, hanging in curtains. It's a blessing that she can't see how close she swings to the floor as she's yanked into her own chair so hard that the back pinches, close to folding in on itself the way that it does when they collapse it to go into the car.

Like a baby bunny backed into a corner, Tilly-Tok blinks with a shaking lip. She's just about pulling herself back into the position when the chair gets pushed. Gravity slaps her against the back.

"What the hell, Tessa?" She neatens up her hair, pushing it out of her face, just in time to be smacked with the remembrance that there is hole in the floor a mere two metres away.

"Stop! The floor could be rotten before we even get there!" She spins, facing back as best she can.

That isn't Tessa!

A scream so loud it could split the plaster from the walls bursts from her.

The pallid nurse pushing her glances down. Her eyes are pure ice and ghosts dance in them.

"Stop!" Tilly grabs the wheels, friction painting a lurid, red line on each of her palms, edged by sludge.

"Enough," says the nurse as the chair stops. She snatches Tilly's thin wrists away with such force that the outlines of their brittle bones clash against each other.

"Let go! That hurts!" Crystal tears spring from the corners of her eyes.

This is unlike anything Tilly has ever been through before. There's being afraid, and then there's being terrified. So scared that your heart isn't just racing, it's a

drumline in your ears. The kind of terror that makes your mouth go dry and your stomach threaten to upheave.

It's an ugly fear. Her hands are trembling in the nurse's grip. Her lower lip wobbles as her mind spins into static. No explanations. Just empty air and the realization that Tessa is nowhere nearby.

Much to her surprise, the squeeze lessens. The nurse steps around to her side and places her hand on Tilly's arm. The blonde's chest rises and falls, arms held close.

Tilly doesn't dare move again, lest the nurse grab her hands again. Tilly's always bruised easily, and there are faint red marks on her wrists where the nurse's fingers had been. The thought of being touched again is . . . too much.

Before her, the floor is starting to sag. The hole was clearly made from water damage, and all of the boards surrounding it have dipped in towards it. A few more years and they'll probably fall down too. If the weight of Tilly's wheelchair doesn't do it today, at least.

Tilly tries to swallow past a lump in her throat, but it doesn't clear. She curls her hands up against her chest, fingers twisting in the fabric of her shirt, trying to ground herself.

It doesn't help.

"Miss," the nurse says in a voice that breathes cold into the air. "If it hurts, we must make it better. Your

myasthenia is our top priority. Perhaps, if correctly treated, we can return you to a state of being where you may contribute to society."

Tilly rears her head, summoning a fire to fight the ice. "I appreciate the attention to detail in your act but . . ." Having readied to teach the cosplayer a thing or two, Tilly finds herself transfixed by something. On the wall there are a set of scratches, carved in scoops that can be from nothing other than fingernails. Her blood runs cold, stopping in her veins the same way that the blood has dried in the dips of the wall, not just at what they mean, but that she can barely make them out . . . through the nurse.

"Hah!" The air catches in her throat. Her fire is doused.

"Now, let's get you all better."

Tilly has been through more procedures than she can count in her short life. From knee jolting traction to straightening her limbs (and proved to make them even floppier) to more needles than a hedgehog's back, she's had people wanting to help her improve for as long as she can remember. The way that nurse just said "let's get you all better" could not have filled her with more dread.

She can see through the nurse. Through her!

That single realization changes everything. This is no cosplayer, determined to be in character for a video, and this is no-one playing a cruel joke. You can't see *through* people.

Not *living* ones, at least.

It feels as if there are wires wound through her body, all of them pulled taunt. Tilly's breath is tangled up in her throat. It's hard to pull in enough air. The dust and mold scent suddenly becomes overpowering. More than ever, she wishes she had brought her anxiety medicine with her. Something to help calm her racing heart would be more than welcomed.

"Some hydrotherapy will do the trick." The nurse starts pushing again.

There's no time to clutch the wheels this time!

Tilly squeals, throwing her arms over the back of her chair as much as she can as it clatters on the exposed beams, barely skimming the rotten edges. Bits of wood tumble away as she starts to slip.

"Childish!" scolds the nurse as if this whole thing is Tilly-Tok's fault. The front caster drops, the janky chair virtually tossing the vlogger out.

And it would have, if not for the cruel clutch of the nurse. She hooks her back in, giving her one last look at the dark descent to the floor below before they reach the other side. A falling plank of wood rattles below.

"What the hell is going on?"

Another nurse opens the corner door before trotting off. Tilly snatches at her apron—anything to avoid being

plunged into that sodden room. Her grip isn't enough, though, and she's in before she can utter another complaint.

The room features three baths, each with battered tarps, ribboned with straps, hanging from the sides.

"Be thankful that you are not of an asylum, and that you came to our select and esteemed surgery. They would have you beaten for such blasphemy."

The floor is thick with rancid water, congealed and of the texture of drool and treacle. Clumps of green algae float on the surface, disrupted only by the ripples in the water where they've opened the door. The lower sections of the walls are near-black with rot, the scent of stagnant water burning at her nostrils. It's a wonder that the entire floor hasn't just caved in beneath them.

Rust clings to the metal features of the tub, dark as dried blood, and Tilly thinks, from the smell of it, that some poor animal must surely have drowned in all this water. It's as if something has died in here and—that's a thought she tries to shake out of her mind for the moment.

She can almost feel the sodden wood sinking beneath the wheels of her chair, as if it's settling like memory foam. More ripples spread out, churning up clouds of black slime within the water. It's enough to make her gag just from the smell. The thought of being in it is unbearable.

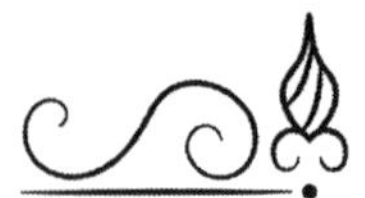

Tilly shrinks into the chair with her head down. She's seen *Supernatural*. She needs . . . iron and salt. There's fat chance of that here, though. She cusses under her breath, hands pressed on her face.

The nurse looks over the chair and reaches down to crank the break on. Narrowing her eyes at her patient, the nurse collects a pipe and thrusts it through the spokes. Tilly peaks through her hands.

Dredging through the slime, the nurse turns on the faucet to the end tub. It spews out a handful of leaves and judders. But then the water begins to come. It spits out, speckling the ivory sides with brown.

Bile rises in Tilly's throat and she spits it into the waterlogged floor where it is lost in swirls of engulfing slime. Her throat—her muscles—her heart; everything burns. And as if that wasn't enough, steam begins to flood the air, stinking of rotten plant matter and sulphur.

The water level is rising, and the door is shut.

# CHAPTER 7.

The merger of Tilly's sniffles and the humming of the nurse make for a twisted lullaby, and it's one that has been played on repeat in this place for years.

The water has finally begun to run clear, but with so much ooze in the bottom it is far from pretty. The stripes are week-old tiramisu, coffee-thick sludge settling under an over-soaked biscuit and ounce upon ounce of insipid brown.

"Please . . ." Tilly's voice is a whisper.

"This is to make you better."

The blue-eyed vlogger leans over, her hand clawing for the pipe in the spoke. Over the arm of the chair, she's inches away—inches that she doesn't have. Her stomach presses on the armrest. The chair creaks, tilting. She's close—so close.

"Uhh!" She has to sit up. Her lungs are maxed out, she can't hold in her breath to squeeze even a millimeter closer. She pants, chest heaving and sweat rolling down her forehead.

Filling her lungs as much as possible, she takes another shot. Her butt leaves the seat, letting her hang over. If she could just straighten her fingers, the bar would be within

reach. Telling her condition to just give in for five minutes off is like telling a cube to roll—whether the nurse agrees or not.

"Come now." The nurse strolls over, addressing Tilly-Tok in that eerie voice full of the best intentions she knows again.

She deflates. "I can't get in that."

"You can and you shall."

"I can't."

The nurse places her hands on her hips. "Which, Miss . . . Do you know, I seem to have misplaced your name . . ."

Tilly hangs over the side, limper than the doll in the other room; one which she now realizes the cruelty of as if she lived it. She would have in this era. Might do yet.

The nurse says, "Your name, Miss."

"Tilly."

"That would be Matilda then."

The word "yes" falls out of Tilly, too weak to nod.

"Then, Miss Matilda, do you not want to get better?" The nurse raises Tilly up, putting her into her place.

". . . I just want to go home."

The faucet screeches in protest at the end of the water.

"And you shall, once we have you rehabilitated." She scoops Tilly up. The looming vision of the heated ooze is the injection of adrenaline she needs.

"How can a damn ghost have this much strength?" She flails her arms, grabbing whatever parts of the uniform she can. The fabric disintegrates in her fingers.

"Wretched thing! You are here to be helped. You will do as required."

Tilly is plonked on the side of the bath. "But look at it!" She sways, close to toppling in.

"Can you not support yourself?"

"What do you think?" Tilly shouts, falling back. The nurse catches her, a moment before she can crack her head on the opposite side of the tub. But not before her hair dips into the foul-smelling water. As she's hauled up, her hair is a mop which drags up every fleck of dirt.

"This could be problematic."

"So," Tilly starts. "I should get back in the chair?"

Being disabled has never really been an issue to Tilly-Tok. That does not make it pleasant, though. For the first time, she has a semblance of gratitude for the paraplegia that affects her legs. It might get her out of this situation, at least.

But then what? Even if Tilly can get the ghost to put her back in the chair, what comes after that? With Tessa seemingly missing – and who knows what has befallen the poor support worker – there's very little that Tilly is going to be able to do. There's still a pipe lodged in the wheel of her chair, after all.

If by some miracle she gets the pipe free and manages to make it out of the room, there's the hole in the floor of the hallway to contend with. It would kill Tilly if she fell through it . . . and she had barely skirted around the hole with the guidance of someone pushing her along. Then there would be the stairs to contend with.

It's a hopeless situation. The dawning terror of that all but smacks Tilly in the face. Her tears begin to fall anew, breath catching in her throat as she struggles to come to terms with what's happening. It all seems so unreal, and yet the chilling truth of the matter is that it's really, honestly happening. The water now pressed up against her neck is proof enough of that. It drips down her back, soaking into the back of her shirt.

The filth in her hair is the least of her problems, as a voice as deep as the plummeting sensation in her stomach filters through the air.

"Nurse, you are required."

A shadow looms in the doorway, catching on her peripherals. Looming at the entrance in a shroud is a

portly man in a gray three-piece suit. His hair is slicker than oil and his eyes as black as polished jet.

It's as though all of the warmth in the room has been stolen, though there wasn't much of it to begin with, before the steam. Tilly is forced to confront the fact that the nurse clinging to her shoulders presently isn't the only ghost lingering in the hospital. Her breath catches and comes out on a noisy exhale. It clouds up in front of her.

For a moment, it's like the world has frozen. The nurse turns slowly to look at the doctor. The doctor stares straight through Tilly, as if he hasn't yet noticed her. And then the nurse digs her fingers tighter into Tilly's shoulders, and time begins to tick anew.

"Certainly, Doctor," the nurse nods. "However, Matilda is being most difficult. Should I send her to isolation? I fear her weakness would not withstand the crop."

The jet eyes lock on to Tilly, ploughing their darkness into her core. "Her condition?"

"Would benefit hydrotherapy, yet her balance remains a concern."

Tilly can hardly believe the situation unfolding around her. A nurse, a doctor, the damned—and she can do nothing about it. Her lip trembles.

The nurse tightens her bony hands on Tilly's shoulders. They are like carved blocks of ice, digging into her flesh.

Dirty smears are left behind, from where the nurse already handled the tarp. It seems as though the grime and sludge doesn't exist to the nurse at all.

Oh, but it exists for Tilly. Even if she could manage to get past the rank smell of it, there's no way to ignore the thick, slimy streaks of sludge tangled in her hair. It brushes wetly against the back of Tilly's neck, like maggots in a tangle of mouldy strings.

"Can you swim, girl?" He demands.

"No," the blonde lies.

"No matter," the doctor says. "Brittle bones are lower in density. She will float. Strap her in."

The nurse swings Tilly sideways and into the tub! Tilly screams—or tries to. Bubbles spew from her and pop on the surface. Water, almost hot enough to scald, rushes into her lungs, tumbling down her throat like hundreds of rusted needles. Her lungs are going to blow up. Her face is out of the water and she gasps. Steam rushes in and it's another wave of needles. The heat—it's unbearable! It's not just in her lungs either. It flushes all over her skin. The goop in the water clings in patches which are as hot as candle wax. Her pale skin blemishes. Even through the murkiness, it's blushing pink.

"It's so hot!" She splutters, spraying the nurse's uniform.

"The perfect temperature. You must become accustomed to it all."

"Strap her in. We have a black woman to deal with," says the Doctor.

Somehow, the blonde—now virtually brunette with water and grime—manages to suck in a breath.

"Tessa . . ." The word falls on deaf ears. Her arms are cast over the side towards the nurse, and the smell hits.

It's such a cloying odour that Tilly can practically feel it settling in her lungs, as if the decay is in the air itself. Her chest is tight, the knot in her throat getting larger and larger with each mouthful of rancid breath. They never should have come poking around up here in this hidden floor. They never should have split up. The rules said not to. Earlier she had followed them, but later, she had to go and let her excitement get away with her.

Tilly wants to go home. She wants to close her eyes and make all of this vanish—but the stench of rotting wood and stagnant water presses in on her from all sides. It's impossible to pretend that Tilly is anywhere but here, struggling in the water. Slime curls around her in great whorls of brown and green, pushing up under the fabric of her sodden shirt. It's thick against her skin. Water drips down her face, stinging her eyes, sour and old when it gets in her mouth.

Tilly gags, struggling to try and get a grip on the front of the nurse's uniform. "No!"

The nurse pushes her away, swishing the water. The movement stings, heat cascading in daggers all over her skin again. Barely a second had passed where her body could cool the temperature around her and any glimpse of coolness is stripped away.

"No!" Her protests don't matter. They're meaningless as the nurse pulls the tarp over the tub. She tugs the straps through one another and ties the top with a string. Only her head is above the tarp and even her perfectly painted face is streaking with sweat. Somewhere in the water her left side of lashes float about, glue melted away.

"This will keep the heat in. Better for the joints." The nurse wipes her hand over Tilly's eye as she pushes against the fabric. Her other lashes are whipped away, but then she is left in the room—alone.

# CHAPTER 8.

Hydrotherapy is not meant to be this disgusting. It was designed to be soothing. Nothing about this situation is remotely relaxing. As long as she stays incredibly still, the heat is painful—but not excruciating. Staying here will do Tilly no good, unless by some miracle, Tessa shows up or the nurse decides to let her go free.

Tilly-Tok fights to get out of the tub, thrashing about as best she can. Her hands beat on the cover but it's as thick as a trampoline. Each time it bounces her off, water slaps against her body—hot and stinking. It puffs up out of the gaps, hitting her in the face with plumes of putrid air.

Rapidly, her arms weaken and sink into the water. They submerge and it isn't long before the ache begins to melt away.

She leans her head back on her hair which squeezes out like a sodden pillow behind her. Tears blink away some of the grime. Tessa isn't back.

"You can do this," she tells herself, taking a few deep breaths in the way that her counsellor used to tell her to do. How she's ever going to tell anyone about this, she has no idea. There is a good chance she's going to need therapy, though—and not the lighter kind she's become settled with lately where she hangs with a good movie

and her friends Ben & Jerry. What kind of therapy can even scratch the surface of this, though?

That's if she even gets out . . .

Tilly summons everything she can, weaving her hand through the gap by her neck. Taking a pause to regain her strength, she thrusts it through and it makes a pop as it frees. A laugh falls from her lips.

"Should have seen that one, Tessa. I bet you'd have a sci-fi reference for that."

Panting, Tilly manages to get her other arm out and drag her body up. A pound more and she might not have been able to squeeze her torso through.

She hooks the straps with her fingers, no longer in any position to care how dirty they are.

Tilly pushes, but nothing happens. The tarp is stuck tight. Desperation threatens to claw at her throat. She has to fight back tears and the urge to give up. Already, her arms burn with effort. The reality of the situation feels almost impossible; a jarring dissonance between normality and the ghosts that have trapped her here in this overheated water. But there's no avoiding the truth of the matter. Tilly is stuck, and if she isn't able to get herself out of this . . . It isn't worth imagining. She gives her head a hard shake, dispelling those morbid thoughts as much as she can, but they're like cobwebs and remnants crawl on her skin. She won't let herself get pulled into that self-destructive spiral.

Now more than ever, Tilly has to have hope. And more than that, she needs to have confidence in herself and her own abilities. Tessa isn't here to help her this time. The weight of the situation is resting solely on Tilly's shoulders.

Tilly tries a second time. This time, her hands slide in the grime, shooting off to the side. Her elbow knocks painfully into the cold water tap. There's a scraping, protesting sound and then the rusted metal snaps neatly in two.

Part of it hits the floor and skitters away. Tilly barely has time to lament that it's not close enough to grab before a massive wave of freezing cold water slams into her. The force is almost enough to sting the back of her neck and her shoulders. The contrast with the near burning hot liquid already in the tub is enough to make her muscles seize painfully and her skin prickle into itches.

If there's an upside to be found, it's only that the water shooting out is clearer than the thick, slime-filled soup she's presently stuck in. It spatters noisily against the tarp. Tilly has to use a hand to push the wet, filthy hair back out of her face.

"Screw urban exploring," she says.

She has to adapt and find a way to get out, that's all there is to it. She starts using her teeth to pull at the ties. The taste is the same one that comes from getting a blast

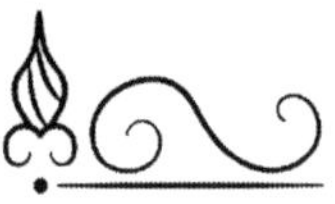

of ash from a bonfire, and it dries every ridge in the roof of the mouth out in the same way. It doesn't matter, though. She can use her teeth and tongue.

Early on in her life, she learned that the tongue was the strongest muscle in the body, and she has used it. Vlogging has been proof of that. If she can communicate her point—who she is—she can do anything. And that includes getting her way out of this. She's an ambassador of her disability, not a victim to it.

Yanking with her teeth, the string is undone.

There's no time to celebrate.

In a heartbeat, she's pushing the ties open. They budge easily now that the string that binds the top hangs. She hauls herself over the side, leaning her torso over. Her legs are little use here, but they keep her balanced at least.

Anyone who can walk probably doesn't think twice about getting out of the bath. Maybe they worry about putting a towel down to catch the drips, but they don't generally worry about falling a couple of feet. Tilly wonders if those people feel the way she does now when they stand on the edge of a rooftop. The outcome of the fall could be the same.

Closing her eyes, she leans further and her weight takes her. Her face scrunches up, waiting for the impact—and it hurts, but not as badly as she expected. She's sliding.

Finally! Something about this awful place has worked in her favor! There is a piece of tarp under the filth and it shifts with her. Her back slaps on the floor, making her whimper. She's determined not to add a single drop more moisture to the room—not a single tear.

Tilly gets onto her elbows and starts crawling to the chair, pulling herself along.

When she reaches the cool metal of the chair, it's better than a cocktail on a pure white beach where the waters are so clear that fish can be seen for miles out. All she needs to do now is to get *into* it.

She turns her back to it, tucking her throbbing spine against the footplates. Putting her hands on them, she pushes herself up. Her bottom raises and she plonks it on the footplates.

Tilly has to stop, then, her whole body trembling from exertion. The muscles in her arms cramp and spasm. This is far more physically exhaustive than anything she does even on her most physically active days. She wants nothing more than to lay down, close her eyes, and pretend that this is all just a bad dream. She's come too far for that, however. Stopping now isn't an option . . . no matter how much Tilly wants to.

Closing her eyes won't get her anywhere, either. Time is working against her, too. Tilly has no idea when the nurse will be back, or what other horrible things might be in store for her. Still, she has to take at least a few

moments to try and catch her breath. The rancid smell clinging to everything makes that a harder task than it might be. Even through the fear, it's hard to ignore the way that the slime feels, caked to her palms and fingers, dripping down the side of her face and the back of her neck.

These clothes are, simply put, ruined. "Alright." She pulls in a deep breath, trying to steel herself. "Come on, Tilly. You can do this."

Her tongue flits across her dry lip and she readies herself for the bigger lift. Floor to footplates is minute compared to footplates to seat.

"Okay, okay, okay." It's almost a chant. Holding her breath, she puts her hands on the seat and forces her way up. Her elbows burn, more than the hydrotherapy which still has her flushed. The edge of the seat brushes against her back, catching on the roundness of her bottom. Her arms quake and she drops.

"Ah!" Her teeth grit. She pushes up again, and there it is! She's on the edge of the seat. She shimmies back and smiles, leaning her head all of the way back to look at the ceiling for a moment. Relief washes over her, better even than sitting under a clean waterfall.

She gets her phone out, and it lights up. There's battery, but no signal.

"Damn it."

# CHAPTER 9.

The pounding in Tessa's head tells her that she is awake long before she opens her eyes. The lids weigh heavy. It must have been one heck of a night out, she thinks, trying to lift her arm to her throbbing temples. It doesn't move. Something has her trapped; probably Maisey asleep on her arm again, she assumes. That girl and tequila . . . Even tequila doesn't usually make her feel this . . . heavy.

"What the heck did I do?" She blinks open her eyes, met with a tiled ceiling. Her vision is hazy, but even as it swirls, there is no doubting that this place is in need of a serious clean up.

"What indeed?" A rasping voice comes from her left. Her body jerks—only to be jolted back. Around her wrist are thick, leather manacles.

"What the—?"

"You are bound. Cease your complaints," the male voice says. It infects her to her core, slithering into her ear as she cranes her neck away.

The pulse in her head drops to her heart and picks up the pace. She goes to sit up, finding that only her neck bends and there is a strap pressing on her chest.

Her whereabouts dawns on her like a sun blazing on precious ice caps. She had been urban exploring, there with one of her best friends.

"Where's Tilly?" Tessa snaps her head to the other side. The man, who wears a gray three-piece suit, has the darkest eyes she has ever seen. The pupils are so wide that the faint ring of brown around them all but blends—nothing to them but burned glass.

No answer comes, only the soft clank of instruments being moved on a side tray. Tessa's eyes widen—the weird treatment room on the second floor. As far as she can recall, they'd just reached the secret roof floor. She was coming down to retrieve the wheelchair and—

"You freaks jabbed me!" Still nothing. "Hey! Are you listening to me?" Her wrists tug against the straps. A couple-hundred years on and they still hold strong.

"You shall be injected again if you do not allow yourself a modicum of decorum. Men are not to be addressed in such a manner, particularly doctors."

Her bottom lip curls down at the sour taste he is giving off. "Excuse me?"

Once again, there is no reply.

Tessa says, "you can't just drug people and tie them down, you creep. This isn't cool!"

Tessa tries to get out more—unsuccessful and completely ignored.

"Look, this isn't right. There's a girl in a wheelchair here who needs my help to get out. This prank is going way too far."

There is a knock and a nurse strolls in. "Doctor," she says.

"Wonderful." The man turns to Tessa. "What plantation are you from?"

The noise that the black woman lets out is close to a hoot—winded by the notion. She chokes out a laugh.

"Is that some sort of tasteless joke? Bitch, I worked in an old people's home with dudes who didn't know better. You, though? You know *12 Years a Slave* was about raising awareness of those atrocities, not a guidebook, right?" Strapped to a table in the presence of two verifiable nutcases probably isn't the best time to get mouthy. The fire in Tessa's soul burns up, though, and it spills out as a scorching flamethrower from her mouth and eyes. The doctor and nurse are made of ice and glance at each other, deflecting her.

"Should I fetch a sedative?" the nurse asks.

The doctor shakes his head. "No, no. She'll hold. She had such energy carrying Matilda but these are designed to

hold the mad. Without inhibitions, they often grow exceedingly strong. Thank you for your report on that."

Tessa grits her teeth. "Who are you people? Do you get your kicks from scaring people? Well, you picked the wrong woman!" She snatches at her restraints with a clang . . . and nothing else.

The jerk makes her whole shoulder burn, all down the length of her arm. It bites into her wrist with a fury like little else Tessa has known. She can barely keep her pained yelp to herself, gritting her teeth to try and bite back the muffled wail.

The nurse takes half a step back. "Gracious! Are you quite sure about the sedative? She seems a vicious creature!"

"Unnccessary."

"It is in the nature of their kind—"

Tessa snaps. "Who in the blue hell do you think you are?"

"Silence!" The nurse snaps.

Tessa's blood is lava, bubbling under the surface of her skin. It mixes with the sedative, eating it up, and bubbling —ready to erupt.

The doctor raises his hand. "She isn't one of them. She holds her sanity. Forgive my informality. I am Doctor N. Garaufis, practice owner and founder of the Investigative

Asylum for Uncouth Aristocracy. You, however, do not fit in here with the invalid and deranged."

". . . What do you mean? A doctor . . ." The words slip away the way her sanity seems to be doing. He might be more corporeal than the nurse, but that doesn't mean he's there. "Am I going insane?"

The nurse folds her arms. "This one does not listen. You have already made your diagnosis have you not, Doctor?"

Tessa struggles to figure out what's going on. She tries to think about what happened leading up to this point; the nurse had appeared, and she had stabbed her with the needle. But what about before that? There had to be some kind of secret to this. Some sort of explanation.

"Her charge must walk. It will be a crowning moment of the institute. No more shadows and secrets."

Those words are familiar. Hadn't that been what Tessa heard while Tilly-Tok was downstairs? Tessa had thought it to be the vlogger at the time, but if that wasn't the case . . . Could it have been these two? But no, that doesn't make any sense. Tilly had seen the nurse out in the courtyard. She couldn't have been in two places at once.

That's when Tessa remembers the shadows that they had spotted on the recording, and sweat lashes at her brow. And then after that, the batteries on everything had started to drain. The phones, the cameras . . . It was as if something was trying to suck the life straight out of the

electronics. It all adds up to one of the most baffling conclusions that anyone could come to. The supernatural.

In any other circumstance, Tessa might laugh at the suggestion . . . but these people act as if they've never stepped into the modern century. Could the hospital really be haunted?

Now that Tessa is thinking about it, that feels almost like the only option available. How else could any of this be happening? She twists, trying to get a better look at the two people who have locked her up. They look human at first glance, but the nurse—she's near-skeletal. Nothing but pale white flesh pulled tight over bones. And the doctor is just unnatural-feeling, as if he's a person but not really a person. Not in the real sense of the word.

And while they look solid enough to begin with, if Tessa squints hard, if the light hits them the right way . . . there's something almost translucent about them. She wonders, would they seem so solid if the room weren't quite this dark? Would they seem so real?

Would they seem more like ghosts?

That thought alone is enough to make Tessa's chest clench. It's followed by a wave of nauseating swill churning in her stomach, as she realizes that Tilly is somewhere in this hospital, alone. She never should have brought Tilly here. Tessa just wanted to give Tilly the best of the best—the same experiences as everyone—the freedom to go and do what she wanted.

This was supposed to be the shining piece of glory on Tilly's vlog. And even beyond the idea of internet fame, it was something that Tessa just honestly really wanted to do. Now, it's some sick re-enactment of the darkest stain in world history.

The thought of it backfiring so horribly as to have ended up in a haunting . . . attacked by ghosts? It's so far away from what Tessa had wanted that it's not even laughable. Tessa can only hope that these spirits or monsters or ghosts—whatever they are—haven't been able to find Tilly yet. Maybe she's had better luck.

That's a thought which is crushed as fast as that needle was sunk into her neck in the following moments, as Tessa becomes more aware of what the nurse and the doctor are saying.

The conversation between the two had faded into the distance but now it's back in full focus; like their sepia world just got painted in.

"Hmph." He offers her a look which curls his lips in an ugly way. "You see my concern."

The nurse nods. "There is indeed too much familiarity between the two."

Did they really think that their efforts will change anything? The sheer disbelief of that statement is almost enough to drown out the fear.

"It will do the girl no good to lean on this crux," the doctor begins, addressing the nurse as Tessa's mouth hangs open. "A servant is one thing but the level of dependency will do her no good. No good at all."

Tessa's insides are a war of hot and cold; the icy realization of her situation against the flaming desire to rip apart Doctor Garaufis' racist ass apart. But . . . how do you do that to a ghost? Ghoul? Spectre? Whatever in all that is unholy this is.

Tessa twists in her bonds, trying once more to break free. This time, it's not the frantic pulling that left her so sore before. It's methodical. A test. That's how Tessa needs to address the situation. One fact at a time.

These people are dead. The hospital is haunted. And she needs to get free.

She tries her legs first. The left one, then the right. A hard shake to try and dislodge the bindings. They don't move. The table gives a clang where they rattle together. It makes the skin pinch. There are going to be bruises forming there in the morning, that's for sure. Morning! Ha! That's if she even makes it that long!

Tessa stops that thought before it can go any further. She can't think about things like that. She can't just give up before she's even tried.

Her arms, then. The same methodical way of testing. Her left one first, but there's not even a little give in the leather. She wiggles her fingers; the binding is tight, but

it's not cutting off circulation. Still, it bites painfully into her wrists.

Tessa tries to move her right arm and—is that a bit of leeway? It is! Not much. Just enough for the leather to not dig so painfully hard against the knob of her wrist.

That little bit of leeway is enough to give Tessa some amount of hope. It becomes the only thing that she focuses on. The rest of the world fades away into the background as Tessa struggles to loosen it more. The psychopathic medical crew keep talking and she eases her hand from side to side.

Somehow, through her daze, the words begin to float together.

"Wait . . ." Tessa pauses. "Are you saying you'll only let me out of here if Tilly walks in here to claim me?" Being treated like a stray on a leash is not something that somebody expects to deal with in the 21st century. In fact, it's downright offensive.

"That is correct."

The leeway comes to an end. Her mouth turns dry. Playing the game might be the last thing that she wants to do, but it might get her out of this. Her and Tilly.

"So, go get her. We can clear this up."

"Get her?" The nurse's teeth show the way sharks do. "That would be counterproductive to the doctor's plans for her recovery."

"She can't walk!"

The Doctor bobs his head. "A disorder of the mind as much as the body."

"No. It's not." The gall of that statement! These people know nothing about Tilly. If they did, they would never make the claim that this was just a mental block. Tessa knows that doctors viewed things differently in the past, but that's just an asinine thought.

Is breaking a bone a disorder of the mind? Losing a limb? Snapping your spine? Clearly not! So, the fact they could look at Tilly and think this was a disorder of the mind is just . . . It's crazy. Not Tilly. And not her, either. It's unlike anything Tessa can stand to listen to.

Her head falls back with a clang on the metal. "I'll never see Stonehurst Asylum in the same light again."

The nurse juts her lip forward. "Stonehurst. I am afraid I do not know it."

"No, it's a movie . . . Look, Tilly isn't sick."

The Doctor strokes his chin. "Mere hypochondria under the cartilage."

"That's not what I mean. You're dead. Look at my clothes. Are these the clothes of your time? Jesus, look at the decay in here!"

He waves a dismissive hand after glancing around. "Perhaps we should offer you your own treatment. You will be of sounder mind to understand then."

"My treatment?" With no way to lash out, her fire begins to recede to an ever-smouldering ember. What replaces it is a cool curl of ice, flowing through her veins like water.

"Quite. A little therapy and we'll note is as Drapetomania."

"Drapeto-what?"

"A condition coined by our American cousins. Cartwright coined it, and Stedman noted it was 'uncontrollable or insane impulsion to wander' as a slave."

"You have got to be kidding me!"

"I quite agree, a ridiculous notion, but one which would go unquestioned."

Tessa's attention is brought to the glint of metal on the tray. "What are you going to do to me, you sick son of a—"

The cold back hand of the nurse slaps across her face like broken glass.

The doctor takes out a pocket watch and flicks it open. "We wait two hours to see if she is claimed. If not—well, it'll come to that."

The pain doesn't just sting; it burns like no slap should. The place the nurse touches stays cold, as if there's something tainted about it. This whole place drips with some sort of disgusting filth, a kind of sick otherness to it . . . but nothing quite so foul as the look on the nurse's face.

It twists up into something cutting, something so chilling that it all but makes Tessa's heart still in her chest. The air turns even colder than it had to begin with. The doctor looks unconcerned with the matter, as if Tessa isn't even a bug worth his time. It's the way he slides the watch back into his pocket, his stark black gaze barely even glancing over Tessa. It's the look of a man who considers this business. Interesting business, perhaps, but business all the same.

The nurse?

Her look is that of someone who takes not only pride in her work but absolute glee in it. There's something about her smile that cuts worse than the back hand ever could. A sort of child-like giddiness at the prospect of Tilly not showing up, at the thought of being able to do something no doubt even more cruel and terrifying to Tessa. She's come across her kind all too often in care. They have a particular dislike for certain people for arbitrary reasons.

They sure as anything don't get into care to actually *care*. And they're bitter, too, just like that smile.

The nurse, more than anything, looks excited to have Tessa strapped down on this table.

And that?

That's God damn terrifying.

# CHAPTER 10.

To think that it was only a couple of hours ago that Tilly was being pushed along the ground floor so that she didn't get grime on her hands. She doesn't think twice about grabbing hold of the wheel rims this time. It is imperative that she gets back to Tessa. How she's going to do that, though, she's not yet quite sure.

"One piece at a time," she tells herself. Tilly-Tok is used to a life filled with planning—where the next disabled bathroom will be, whether the accommodation she's chosen has access, if she is allowed to film in the venues, and down to the smallest details like whether her wheelchair will fit through the doors, particularly in the older buildings. Yes, her life up until this point has been about meticulous planning. And it is exactly that which has become a hindrance. Sometimes you just have to go with the flow and take things as they come. It doesn't stop the pang in the pit of her stomach from bubbling up, though.

She has to brush it off. She's here now. Things don't always go as intended. She's just going to have to roll with it—one turn of the spokes at a time.

Tilly pushes herself out into the corridor and lets out a huff of breath that had been captured in her lungs. There's no nurse in sight. Not one single ghostly apparition.

There is, however, the hole in the floor.

She curses, edging towards it all the same.

The chair begins to go under its own weight and she has to grip the metal bars on the wheels. It doesn't take a physics genius to work out that the floor is sagging. It's as though there is a vortex in the middle; a black hole, unseen to the naked eye, sucking everything in without prejudice. Sodden slats, floorboards, vlogger—it's just all fodder to the fall.

Tilly swallows and the lump drags as it goes down her throat, made up as much by revolting grime than nerves.

She's come over once already today . . .

The slope down to the beams is going to be tough to keep control over. Once the wheels are set in motion, it will pull on its own weight. That could mean drifting to the sides. Tilly looks between them. Her right side has the bigger hole—the one that would send her plummeting down. Her left is smaller, but it would throw the chair sideways. She would be stuck unless, of course, the impact dissolved the sodden floor.

Assessing it doesn't have any consequences, though. If the chair slips, there is going to be very little control over which way it goes.

Tilly wipes her hands on the front of her pinafore dress, one at a time. She inhales, then exhales—making herself as miniscule as humanly possible. Then she takes

a deep breath and begins to slowly make her way towards the hole. The best bet she decides is to just go straight along the centre and try to keep steady.

Easier said than done, as she quickly figures out. The wood sags beneath the wheels of the chair. As soon as she starts down the sloping beams, the chair begins to move under its own weight, dragging itself forward.

Tilly's heart is pounding like a jack-hammer. It feels like her lungs have stopped working completely. The air isn't just trapped in her, it's completely gone. She can feel the chair trying to veer towards the big, gaping hole. The vortex in the floor that wants to just completely swallow her alive.

Her fingers ache. She's never gripped the wheels this tight before. Tilly struggles to keep it on the right track, leaning as much to the left as she can, trying to counter the chair's constant drag towards the break in the floor.

And then, miraculously, she's over it. The floor is almost solid. Tilly lets up on her grip—and instantly regrets it as the chair goes backwards. The floorboards must still be warped here; they drag her backwards, straight towards the pit.

"No!" The word is almost punched out of Tilly. She scrambles for the wheels again, desperate not to let her journey end here. The slime on the wheels makes them even harder to grip than normal. They slide against her

palms. The wheels half dip into the hole, the chair leaning traitorously backwards.

Tilly throws her weight forward, giving the wheels one last desperate, violent jerk.

They go forward. The chair steadies out. Tilly doesn't stop until she's nearly halfway across the hall, and on certainly solid ground. The adrenaline all but bleeds out of her. She sags, wilting like a flower left out in the heat for too long. Her entire body aches.

She struggles to catch her breath, but a new wave of fear hits her. She can't stay here.

Tilly propels the chair to the stairs and then slams on the break. This is an entirely new challenge that she must face.

"Come on," she tells herself. "You can do this. One step at a time."

Very carefully, Tilly tries to slide herself down out of the chair. It's the opposite of her earlier struggle. She manages to plop down onto the foot plates, and then onto the floor. But it's absolutely nothing compared to the journey that still waits for her.

Tilly has to scoot over to the top of the stair case. It seems daunting; three times as long as it really is.

"It's just like any other challenge," says Tilly. "When this is all over . . . I'm never going to a second floor again."

And then she starts moving, butt bumping her way down to the bottom floor, one step at a time. She lifts her legs down a step, then gets on the one above them, takes a breath and repeats. Legs down, bottom down, knees bent, breathe. Legs down, bottom down, knees bent, breathe. And again. Legs down, bottom down, knees bent, breathe. It's slow and each drop has her flinching more and more. One hop at a time. One step by one step. Each bump, more painful than the last.

But there! The end is in sight!

Tilly starts counting them. She's five from the bottom; footsteps are feint in the distance. Four from the bottom; they're getting closer. Three from the bottom—and suddenly, bony, sharp hands are grabbing her under the arms, stopping her descent. This is another nurse, frog-faced and with hairs on her chin.

"No," Tilly all but wails. "Get off of me!"

It's not the same nurse as before, but her eyes are just as glossy. There's no question about it. She's as dead as all the others—practically made of glass.

"You must be the problem patient I have been hearing about. This just will not do at all."

They turn and start back up the stairs.

"Tessa! Tessa!"

"Shouting will not get you what you want, young lady!"

Tilly sags, exhausted from her escape attempts to bat her arms harder than a fly landing on her decrepit shoulder. "I just want to go home."

"I know, dear, but you must get well first," says the nurse. She carries Tilly back up the steps and into a room.

Tilly recognizes it instantly from Tessa's descriptions earlier: it's the doll room.

The nurse puts Tilly down on the bed and gives her a condescending pat on the head. "There you are, my dear. You wait here. I have others to attend to."

And then she just fades out of the room, there and then gone. Tilly is left alone. Everything hurts. Her muscles burn. She's exhausted to a point where she could close her eyes and sleep. A nice strong cup of coffee or even an energy drink would not be passed up right now. Especially an energy drink . . .

There's none of that here, of course.

It's just Tilly and the doll.

She looks at it; the glass eyes, the childlike body and vacant expression, the moth-eaten satin dress. Her final assessment is, "you're freaking creepy."

The doll, thankfully, does not answer. At this point, she wouldn't be shocked if it did.

# CHAPTER 11

Tessa's wrists burn from trying to free herself from the bonds, and the more she breathes, the tighter the chest strap feels. Lurid, red lines are dented onto her wrists, close to cutting through. The kiss of cold in the air might be a blessing, even as it turns her fingertips numb. If it's affecting her this much, she has to worry about what it is doing to Tilly.

That's when she hears the girl. It's through the heavy door, but that was certainly her name! Not her voice, though. Someone else's. There's a brief wonder in Tessa's mind—how many ghosts are currently drifting around this place? More than just the two that are in here with her, clearly.

But then Tessa comes to an even brighter realization. She has to at least let Tilly know that she was alive!

"Tilly!" She heaves her head up as much as the restraints allow, letting them cut into her shirt. The more she thrashes, the tighter the restraints seem to feel. "Tilly! Call for help!"

"Hush!" The nurse knits her brow. She looks more and more angry by the moment. Her expressions are ugly and soured.

"Tilly! Tilly!" Tessa doesn't listen, outright ignoring the nurse. This is a chance that she can't pass on. Tessa has to get her friend's attention.

The nurse steps around the table, barely squeezing through and coming to the table. Tessa calls so loud that her vocal cord stings—until the nurse clamps her tongue with the dirty forceps. Her tongue is nipped and pulled out between her lips, making her gag the way that having to do all of those throat swabs at work did.

"Nyehhh!" The last time her tongue was this far out, she was sixteen, getting a piercing that she managed to hide for almost five years. The pinch bites. Is she trying to yank her tongue right out of her head? It's surprising how far it extends before the Doctor speaks.

"Nurse, please. I just sterilized those," he says. Judging by the bump of her brow, Tessa isn't the only one who didn't think he did a good enough job. It's covered in thick grime; rust that flakes off against her tongue, and the same thick layer of black that seems to cling to everything in this place.

Even if the sensation of having her tongue wrenched so far out of her mouth wasn't enough to make her gag, the taste was enough to do the trick. Tessa had never had anything so foul in her entire life.

"With all due respect, Dr. Garaufis, she's going to wake the residents with all of this commotion."

"Not a concern." He extends his hand for the spit-slicked instrument. "Her calls won't penetrate the roof area. It is well insulated, lest they are heard out here."

"Should we take such a chance? This work is so very important, as you said." The nurse squeezes and gives a slight twist in a way that will surely have the pinkish flesh turning into a swollen purple blimp in her mouth by the morning.

"I appreciate the concern." He beckons again and she releases, handing them over.

Tessa retracts her tongue, scraping the grime off of her teeth. It clings to her front teeth in great, disgusting globs. The flavor is never going to leave her, no matter how much she brushes or gargles. She curses, and this time it is the doctor who glares.

He steps over to the table, not quite touching it but making his presence known. His eyes are so dark, like glinting empty pits in his face. Staring at them too long makes Tessa's chest hurt, and the knot in her throat get even tighter. "Such language is most unladylike. What we do here—"

"—Is insane!" The rattling of the straps starts up again to no avail. The claw-like hand slams down on hers. This time, the doctor, who Tessa likes less and less by the second despite having a very low starting point, does not react beyond a glance.

The nurse's grip is intense. It feels like a clamp around Tessa's wrist. Sharp, jagged nails bite into her skin. For as cold as the air in this room is, it's nothing compared to the frigid chill of the nurse's skin. It feels like she's been standing in a walk-in freezer for the last few hours.

Tessa tries to jerk away but can't. "Let go of me!"

The nurse ignores her. She looks at the doctor instead. "What would you have me do with her, then?"

The doctor looks Tessa over. She feels like a lab specimen. His gaze practically cuts through her, deeper than anything else that Tessa has ever known. Whatever he sees in her, he must not like. His mouth curls up into the start of a rather cruel-looking grimace.

"Since we have a considerable amount of time, allow me to perhaps work on your more obvious condition." He picks up a scalpel. The blade is just as filthy as the forceps had been, the metal of it coated with a thick layer of rust. It looks no less sharp for all of the filth.

"Whoa. Whoa. Whoa. Hold up." Tessa shakes her head, trying desperately to come up with a valid enough reason that might dissuade the doctor. "You don't need to do anything with that, alright? Just – put it back down."

"A little blood-letting will help you to release the dark feelings of which you hold. This method has seldom failed me in the past."

He places the scalpel against the inside of her forearm. The blade presses, denting the skin until—

"Ahh!" A stream of red begins to trickle from Tessa's arm as he drags the blade through her like a steak knife on a blue sirloin. "Stop!"

The nurse is there with a tray, silver and kidney shaped. It's surprisingly clean—at least until her blood rolls into it—which is more than she can say for the instrument that sinks into her again and again. Arching her neck back until it feels as though her skull is grinding into the table, she tries to think of anything else—anything to keep her mind somewhere else. The first thing her mind latches onto is the what she wants to do first when she can get out of here. The craving for chicken nuggets hits her, followed by the more practical desire to book in for a tetanus shot. Her teeth grit. He really isn't easing up.

"Focus, focus," she grunts to herself, closing her eyes as the nurse's joy seeps into the air like a disease. There is no doubt that the nurse is greatly enjoying this.

She's going to have ketchup—no, mustard—both. She's going to deserve both! And a movie? What movie is she going to watch? Certainly not horror. No damn ghost stories, no matter what Tilly recommends. It needs to be something fun.

The knife cuts particularly hard, close to her elbow. "Ahhhh-aaa-Adam Sandler! Ben Stiller! Owen Wilson! Jack Black! Aaahh! Steve shitting Coogan!"

The droplets running down her arm slow, and the ache remains in fierce slices, but the blade is out. With a sweat so cold it might freeze on her cheeks and set in her dark hair, Tessa opens her eyes and her mouth. Her arm is a wrap of interlocking ribbons that have her breaths turning to wheezy dips of her chest. Crimson stains the hands of the doctor as he wipes the scalpel on a rag.

In a flicker he's disappeared and reappeared half a foot backwards. He turns to the cupboard and extracts a dropper. The bottle is brown and the pipette top close to cracking; it's rubber seal crusted with age. A liquid the color of dried oranges fills it and a droplet hangs from it as he brings the tincture over. The bleeding woman tries to slink away. It's not going to happen, though.

"Iodine for the cuts."

She chews her lip, wanting to point out that he was the one who unnecessarily made them. "You can't use that anymore," she says in a voice as weak as her arm feels.

"Nonsense." The iodine is squirted across her arm and the moment it hits the pain strikes up again. It's a match lighting and catches the sparks on dry leaves—she isn't going to cry out this time, though. He isn't getting that satisfaction; or more precisely *she* isn't. The nurse has been swirling the blood in the tray the way connoisseurs

do with a full-bodied wine. And her attention has absolutely nothing to do with blood sugar or "vapors".

"Sick bitch," Tessa mutters. The ice-blue eyes tilt up very slowly, the way marbles do out of dark corners along with a child's giggle in a horror movie.

She tilts her unholy hat along with her neck which seems all too stretched, curling her lips into a smile so tight and false that it seems more like a slanted crack in her face.

"The little black bird thinks it can outfox her betters."

"Muriel, let the poor creature be. Her letting will have been quite the ordeal."

The nurse sneers. "Her kind do not have the same feeling as us. It is what makes them such good slaves, available for beating."

Tessa spits in her direction. It slaps her in the face with a splat and she curls her hand to wipe it away with a grimace.

The bloody arm tenses. "I bleed like anyone else you uneducated, racist cow. White, Black, Asian, Hispanic, Native—all bleed the same. Even your tiny brain must have seen that in your role."

The doctor concurs with a nod. "Quite true. Though, there are biological differences, and the standard

variation between genders, the core elements remain intrinsically linked and systematically the same."

The look the nurse gives is as crisp as the crack of her knuckles as she grips the tray of blood. After a few deep breaths of the rotting air, she purifies further. There is a clang as she pushes it onto the side and folds her arms, pursed lipped.

"Well then," the nurse starts. "If they bleed the same, perhaps she should be used to further our experiments. An unclaimed woman of no note will hardly be missed."

Tessa can't believe that her words have been twisted as badly as the ideals in this place. The idea that this building was a mere doctor's surgery is laughable. If only people knew what atrocities must have gone on here! Then again, the rich probably did.

The doctor rubs his chin with a smear of blood. He looks at his watch and nods. "If unclaimed, we experiment on her in the name of research. Our patrons will be grateful of our progress, and God will bless your sacrifice." His hand lays on Tessa's cheek—as frosty and dead as the futures of those who resided here.

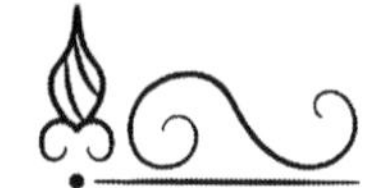

# CHAPTER 12.

The room is getting even darker as Tilly sits on the edge of the bed, aching from the top of her golden hair to the perfect manicure on her toes. She releases a sigh which hangs heavy in the stagnant air. Without a window to look through, the room is even darker, to the point that it takes a few moments for her to adjust her eyes once the door is shut.

“This isn't the kind of adventure I wanted.” She would cry but she's all out of tears. Besides, her body twinges so much that the idea of moving a muscle, even flexing a tiny little duct in the corner of her eye, is too much.

Today she has spent more energy than she even knew she could have. A person cannot be entirely void, though, and it seems that every gap within her is crammed tight with tension and a dull ache—apart from her back, which has lightning rods striking in it every few seconds. She supposes that she should be grateful for the fact she's alive, but right now it doesn't feel much like a blessing. It's hard to imagine what she wouldn't give to stand up and walk out of this abandoned hell hole right now.

Where her wheelchair is, she hasn't got a clue. Even if she did, what would she be able to do about it? For the first time in a long time, Tilly feels anything but

empowered. Her head hangs low. And that is where she stays for well over an hour.

The world has turned quiet, like the ghostly footsteps no longer exist. The bitterness in the air tells another story, though. It's just another callous trick of the horrid place.

Suddenly, there's a wail! Tilly-Tok bolts up straight, bringing herself to attention. It's a frightful noise, one which seems to cut through every fiber of her being. It starts out like a growling in the throat, the kind of noise that people who have trouble with their voice boxes make, then it becomes louder. The vibrations of it reverberate around the room, painting the walls with pain anew that clings to the vlogger's heart. There's no doubt about the fact it is another person—the question on her lips is whether they are alive or dead. On second thought, she probably doesn't want to know.

The noise dissipates, leaving remnants of it decorated all around. The heartache clings to everything in the place, much like walking through cobwebs. No matter how much the young blonde tries to flick them away, the invisible strings tie her up in lament and settle on her long after they have physically disappeared.

It isn't long before the sound starts up again—followed by another; the clip-clop of the nurse's shoes. Tilly-Tok's stomach churns so hard that it could turn milk into butter. The steps are quite clearly about to go to the

wailing woman, but will they come to the room she is in as well?

Mouth turning so dry it's like chewing on sand, her heartbeat starts up in her ears. There is a key in a lock, followed by a twist of metal and the swinging of a door. Tilly keeps her eyes tightly closed, until she is absolutely positive that the door is not hers.

The wailing grows louder until it's grating at the back of Tilly's skull. She presses her hands over her ears, squeezing
in . . . but the sounds still drill their way in.

"It's for your own good, Mrs. Riley. You must learn to speak properly."

There's a clap of something—and it doesn't take long to decipher what it is as a higher pitch squeal emanates after.

"Oh God . . ." Tilly's breathing speeds up. They're beating the poor girl. She can only imagine what for. Because she can't speak is the answer, she supposes, but why is another question. She's a married woman, that much Tilly can deduce from her title. In those times, surely that meant she was fully able when she walked down the aisle. In a time of freak shows and curiosities there was little chance of marrying for something as meaningless to them as love.

*Crack!*

The cry is equally loud, extending until the voice breaks.

"I must do this, for your own good. I want you to be well, my little dove. Now, I'll tell you again, Mrs. Riley, you must learn to speak properly. Ask me to stop and I shall do so."

Silence . . .

And then—

*Crack! Crack! Crack!*

Three hits in fast succession.

The noise lessens; cracks continuing but wails drifting out along with the woman's consciousness. Tilly can't just leave it. It's almost as if she knows that person. Misjudged, injured, trapped—she may as well.

Her tongue searches her mouth for words. "Leave her alone! She can't do it; do you hear me?" she calls out. Even as she does, the words—the very syllables themselves—fight to stay in, clinging to her mouth and desperately clutching at her lip. She manages to spit them out, though, and for a long moment there's no sound of the offending instrument. It's just whimpers.

That's when it strikes Tilly. Exhaustion aside, she must get downstairs. Otherwise, it could really end up being her that gets the belt next. The thought is enough to make bile rise at the back of her throat. With only half of

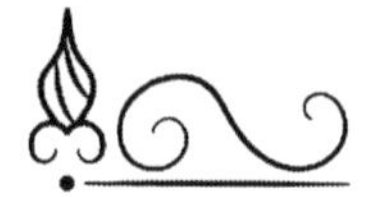

a plan formed, Tilly begins to bang her fist against the wall behind her bed. It makes every joint in her hand throb and ache.

"Nurse, nurse," Tilly shouts. She bangs both fists next. "Nurse!"

There's the *click-clack* of woman's heels. A ghostly nurse, different from before, opens the door. "Cease that endless racket." The lines of her face aren't quite so severe, but her eyes are just as pitch black. "What is the meaning of this, miss? I hope you have a good reason for disturbing so many of our patients."

"I'm sorry," says Tilly, trying her best to sound like a meek, mild-mannered patient. The fact that she's so exhausted helps. "I just wasn't sure how else to get your attention. I can't get up and go to the door on my own. I need a wheelchair to move."

"Ah. Yes, the girl who cannot walk." The ghost's expression softens, just a touch. This one is more portly than the nurse who strapped Tilly into the tub. "And now that you have my attention, do you truly have anything worth saying?"

"The doctor," says Tilly. She pauses, mind spinning as she tries to rapidly form a plan. It feels like she's strapped into the world's worst amusement park ride. "He says that I'm supposed to get medicine from the pharmacy."

The nurse gives a long-suffering sigh, turns on her heel, and leaves. For a moment, Tilly thinks that her con was

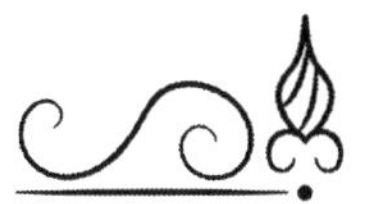

ignored—at least until the clacking of heels is accompanied by the rattle of ancient wheels rolling over cracked wooden floors.

The portly nurse returns, wheelchair in tow. Without so much as a word of warning, the nurse scoops Tilly up and plops her into the chair. A moment later, the restraints are sliding into place.

Tilly swallows, hard. Without even trying, she knows that there's no way to get out of these holds. It's awful, because as much as Tilly wants to move on her own, she knows that at this point, she's so exhausted that the restraints are the only thing keeping her in the chair as it's bounced down the stairs.

Unlike Tessa, the nurse is uncaring of how much Tilly gets jostled about. There's no doubt that the restraints will leave bruises behind. Just one more throbbing ache to add to the rest of the collection. She winces and whimpers down every step.

As they hit the bottom floor, there's a chilling sound. Someone screaming—only this time, it's not an unfamiliar, ghostly wail. It's Tessa.

Tilly's head snaps in the direction of the sound. It comes again, a second time. A pitiful, wailing shout.

The nurse chides her, "Don't be so nosy, miss. Just as you wish your affairs to be private, so do all those who have come here for treatment. Their families pay well for it."

They pass the treatment room where Tessa's boots stick out at the end of the table. In a flash it's easy to see that Tilly isn't the only one strapped in like an old aristocrat in a corset.

Tilly's heart is pounding. The nurse pulls her into the pharmacy, leaving her just inside of the door before going over to one of the ancient shelves. The nurse pulls one of the brown glass bottles from the shelf and shakes three sun-bleached tablets into her palm. They might have been green, years and years ago. Now, they're so old that when the tablets are then transferred into a dirty glass, they break up like dropped chalk sticks.

"Here." The nurse turns to face her. Just thinking about putting her mouth on that filthy glass is enough to make Tilly want to barf. It's even worse when she realizes that the pills could be literally anything. Who knows what they'll do to her?

"No," says Tilly, quickly shaking her head. There's no way in Hell that Tilly is going to let those pills go down her throat.

The nurse's expression sours. "You have been doing well today, Miss Matilda. Do not start being difficult now."

"I . . . I can't take that," says Tilly. She struggles to come up with a plausible reason that won't just have those bony fingers shoving the pill down her throat. "It's the doctor! He changed my prescription earlier today. So—so I can't take that, you see? It's not the right one anymore."

The nurse narrows her eyes at Tilly for a long moment, as if weighing the possibility of that being true.

The woman sighs again, seemingly a habit of hers, and a rush of cloudy, visible air exits from her mouth. She sits the glass of pills down on the counter. It sends up a little puff of dust.

"We must show our new employees how to properly communicate these things. The nurse working with him today should have informed me of the changes. Wait here, miss. I will go see what the doctor has decided is best fitting for your needs." The nurse gives what might have been an attempt at a reassuring pat on Tilly's shoulder. The touch is cold enough to make Tilly shudder.

Then the nurse steps around the wheelchair and back into the hall. The *click-clack* of her heels fades into muffles.

Finally, Tilly is alone once more. Her brief victory celebration is quickly crushed out by the realization that her phone still has no signal. Worse yet, the battery is almost dead. If they're stuck in here too much longer, there will be no chance that Tilly will be able to call for help.

Frantically, she begins looking around the pharmacy, trying to find anything that might help sway the tides of this haunting in her favor. Tilly-Tok needs to find a way to reach Tessa.

She needs to.

# CHAPTER 13.

Screw it. Tilly's in a wheelchair and she knows how to use it. She's gotten down one floor with her innovation and this one is a lot smoother.

She clutches the wheels on the front of the hideous wheelchair and gets moving. She practically bursts into the corridor. Tilly's eyes scan the hallway, glad to realize that there are no ghostly figures drifting about.

"I'm coming, Tessa," she sighs out, pushing her body heat into the air and getting a move on. "What are they gonna do that they haven't already? I'm all good. I get Tessa, we go home, maybe we even torch this place."

That is a very satisfying thought. In her mind's eye, Tilly can already picture it. The flames dancing off of the charred walls of the building, the smoke curling thick and heavy up into the air. It's so far out of the way, no one would come and try to put the fire out until it was far too late, and the building was burned to nothing but smouldering cinders on the ground.

Talk about a goal to work towards!

The chair rolls, but after a few feet, it's slower than she's used to. Between the weight of the old thing and the slime pouring through from the hydrotherapy room above, it's draining her as fast as a TV remote's batteries

with Tessa's channel hopping. It's at the other end of the building but with the pipes from the hydrotherapy room still gushing, there's a sheet of rain falling down from the ceiling and a puddle extending down the corridor. There's an inch of sludge at the lip of the ever-growing flow, but after that, it's clear. This floor isn't going to last too long. How long, is another matter. It could be minutes or hours. By sunrise, though, it will unquestionably be gone —and if they don't get out of there, so will they.

Tilly needs to figure out her next set of plans—and fast. If she waits around too long, there will be no way out but a sudden drop . . . or at the end of one of the nurse's needles. Just the thought of it makes Tilly's stomach flip, an uncomfortable lump forming in her throat. Her arms are burning from the effort she has to use to keep the chair going at a decent pace. Her fingers ache from how tightly she has to hold the large wheels. Even her shoulders have started to throb—the tires set further forward than the build of the modern chair that Tilly is used to.

It's harder to move it with each passing moment. The slime on the floor isn't helping. Exhaustion crests and falls in Tilly like waves lapping at a shoreline.

Voices bubble up from the stairs, gurgling. Tilly pushes as fast as her hands can spin the spokes. There's no way she is going to be able to reach Tessa, though. Tilly has to try something else. For now, at least. The goal is to give the nurses the slip until she's able to come up with a different, better, more proactive plan.

She swings into the nearest room and uses the chair to knock the door shut. It goes with a hefty wallop, even with the water buffering it. The sound seems to echo in the quiet of the ancient building, lingering in Tilly's ears like a thunder clap. Rain from the floor above, thunder from the door closing. All this storm is missing is the lightning bolt. Hopefully, that one will stay gone.

The room must have belonged to the nurses. It's built so they could have stayed overnight, at least one nurse always around to check on the patient after the sun went down. An old bed is pressed against one wall, the sheets on it moth-eaten and covered in a thick layer of filth. There must have been a pillow at one point, but it's long gone—lost to looters or time or something else entirely.

A table is pressed beside the bed, just as filthy as everything else. A once-ornate vase sits on it, filled up with long-dead flowers. They've almost preserved themselves; the rose petals crisp and curled inward, long devoid of color, and the leaves so brittle they might as well be made of tissue paper. A well-timed gust would destroy them, were anyone to open up the bar covered window.

The other side of the room has a large cupboard pressed to the wall. The wood that it's made from is half rotted, water stains dark on the wood. The doors are warped from moisture building up in the air, so that they don't seal up quite the way that they should. There's so much rust on the knobs of the cupboard, it would surely stain the hands of anyone to touch them.

Holding her breath, she leans her head towards the door. There are footsteps at the end of the corridor. *I swear*, she thinks, *if I ever hear a kitten heel again, I'll go crazy*—though that would place her somewhere like here, so maybe not.

The *click-clack* of heels on the floor enter the pharmacy and then come out. The nurse has no doubt realized that Tilly is missing. This is bad. Till had been hoping that her ploy might buy her a little bit of extra time. Clearly, she hasn't been moving fast enough.

"Matilda?"

Even from the other side of the door, her heart plummets. Tilly looks down and sucks back in the breath she let out earlier; sharp and void of its former heat.

Tire tracks. The chair has left them. The thin rims may have slipped easily through the murky water, but that curb of dirt. Well. There are hundreds of tiny, v-shaped arrows chasing the chair in filthy sludge. If the debris and goop dragged and left these pointers at the door . . .

The voice chills the air again. "You are not allowed to be in there, Miss. Matilda!"

She's coming.

# CHAPTER 14.

Through the slip of opening where the warped cabinet doors don't quite connect, Tilly watches the nurse step into the room. Throwing herself onto the floor and scrabbling into a cupboard is something she never thought would be the best option—here she is, though.

The nurse's lips are pursed, her hands on her hips. Her gaze sweeps about like a pivoting security camera, clearly expecting to find Tilly—but the young woman is safely stowed away inside the ancient, wilting cabinet, really hoping that it doesn't collapse on top of her.

The cherry-tinted wood is sodden in spots. The moisture from the rain and constant exposure to the elements has left it not completely steady. If Tilly moves too fast in one direction or the next, the whole cupboard is going to topple over. Then not only will her hiding spot be revealed, but she'll likely end up being even more hurt than she already is.

For once, being still is a good thing.

Getting into the cabinet had been an entirely new sort of challenge. There is something wrong about willingly tossing yourself onto the ground at a height that will bruise. No time for bumping down the footplate. Besides, this chair has big wheels at the front and nothing to grip on the descent. Her choices were under the bed, or in

here. And she's certain that it's also the only thing keeping her from getting a throat shoved deep with crumbling pills and poked with needles as rusty as wet iron.

The nurse puts a hand on the back of the wheelchair. She clicks her tongue. "Orderlies are always leaving things in the wrong room. One of these days, we're going to have to get some people working here that actually know what they are doing! It does not take a genius to know that they should not be leaving equipment in this room."

The nurse gives another sweeping look about the room and leans forward, bracing her hands against the wheelchair.

"Matilda, if I find out that you have absconded with our orderly or any of those hysterical residents . . ." The nurse trails off, but the warning is clear.

Tilly bites her lip, struggling to keep her breathing silent. This is it. This is the moment that will either make or break her escape. The seconds seem to tick past like molasses dripping in winter. The nurse looks about with shrewd, empty eyes. She huffs, clearly deciding that there's no one lurking about in the room, and shaking her head.

She tugs the wheelchair backwards, out of the room with her. The wheels rattle, the chair cracking noisily

against the side of the door. Battered beyond fixing, it only closes partway behind her.

Still, Tilly stays quiet, curled up small in the wooden cupboard. It's mostly empty, though a stray quilt, hand stitched and moth-eaten, has been shoved into the far back of it, along with a ghastly-looking needle. When the nurse doesn't come back into the room, and no more calls of "Matilda" are heard echoing in the halls, Tilly leans forwards. She presses gently on the wood, half-expecting to see it dissolve. Even doing that has her pulse starting up anew in her aching limbs. It's almost tempting to lean back on that quilt for an hour or two. Maybe she would have leaned back and given up—if it weren't for Tessa.

Whimpering, she leans harder and tumbles out.

Tilly hits the floor with the force of someone twice her size, near dead weight and panting. Her knees throb and ache, palms stinging where they've slapped against the floor and slid outwards. Her chin rests on the grimy planks with her butt in the air in the world's most uncomfortable yoga position. She's never wanted a hot shower and a tumbler of pink gin so badly before in her life.

For a moment, she just stays there like that on the floor, her face so close to the grime that the acrid scent burns at her nostrils. Gross.

Tilly's hair is filthy, all tangled and twisted up. She stares out through the mess of dirty blonde strands,

trying to figure out what her next plan of action should be. The syringe, filled with several layers of waxy-looking ooze over amber fluid, has rolled out with her. She pockets it, careful not to spike herself.

A scream splits the air. It's Tessa.

It looks like Tilly doesn't have time to sit around and try to piece things into place. She takes a deep breath and starts to crawl towards the door. The floor in here is dusty. Grit cakes to her palms—but it seems as though it might soon be washed off by the puddle pooling its way in. Slowly, leery that a nurse might be waiting in the hallway, Tilly peeks out into it.

There's no sign of the nurse, or the wheelchair. Tilly lets out a relieved breath. "Alright. Just have too . . . Jesus . . . figure out where Tessa's at now. . ."

The answer comes in the form of another scream. Is that sound coming from the right? Tilly thinks that it must be. Still in the horrid treatment room.

"Guess that's my answer," she says, with a huff. Considering everything that's happened to Tilly so far, it seems almost ridiculous to hope that Tessa's doing any better. And yet that's exactly what Tilly finds herself doing, hoping that maybe Tessa's in a little bit better shape. Aside from their friendship, she's the ticket out of there.

Tilly has to try and stay positive . . . right? That's something her therapist has said before. Speaking of,

there's going to be no end to the amount of therapy that Tilly's going to need after this—though, maybe she shouldn't fill her in on exactly what has happened here. That could result in her being on some strong and unpredictable meds for real.

With a little difficulty, Tilly uses her shoulder to push the door leading back into the hallway the rest of the way open. The hinges creak. Again, she freezes and holds her breath, waiting for someone to come scoop her up like they did before.

Nothing.

Nothing but the pounding of her own heart and the occasional hiss of wind pushing in through the widening cracks in the building.

Tilly starts to crawl out into the hallway. The sound had come from the right, so that's where Tilly's going to try and get to as well. The slick grime on the floor makes it harder for Tilly to keep herself balanced. It's like trying to pull herself through a vat of curdled pudding. Her elbows slip and she shudders to pull them back to place.

There's a rumble behind her, followed by a series of bangs, and the curtain of water gives way to the marbled sky. Water, stagnant for years, rushes in, pushing her back two feet and slicing her ankle on a nail.

She yelps.

If the blood is flowing, she can't see it. In a matter of seconds, the flood is caked so thickly to the bottoms of Tilly's palms that they, too, slide and slip about as she tries to pull herself forward. The wet leaves and debris are so thick beneath her nails that she can actually feel the pressure of it. A foul scent permeates the air, drifting down from the crashing fall of water still pouring out of the gaping hole above.

Even more than the fear, there's a constant surge of disgust lingering in the back of Tilly's mind. It makes her throat itch, and her stomach twist into continuously unsettled waves. It surges up in her; a wave of nausea hits her, bile sour on the back of her tongue. She has to fight to gag it back. And yet there's nothing she can do but keep going.

To the right.

For Tessa . . .

# CHAPTER 15.

"Two minutes left," announces the doctor. He taps his watch with one finger, sending a curiously loud click into the air—loud because there is nothing else beyond the horrid place. A few minutes ago, there was a rumbling crash, and since then there's been nothing. No birds, no wind, nothing.

And that means no sign of Tilly.

Fear as cold as a shattering glacier shoots through Tessa. She's almost too exhausted to keep trying to break free of her bonds. It's not as though she was making any fast progress, and the more she struggles, the more that the painful slices in her arm burns. Some of the cuts are still seeping blood, and now her wrists are too, in beads along the friction marks. It drips hot and wet around the curve of her arm, staining the table beneath it.

"You can't seriously be planning on doing this," says Tessa. "Just let me go! There's—you aren't going to accomplish anything here, alright?"

How are you supposed to reason with a ghost that doesn't realize he's dead? How are you supposed to reason with an absolute maniac like this?

Not easily, that's for certain. In her movies, there's a twist of fate or a comrade to save the day. This? This is

real. There's zero chance of a maintenance man checking in just in the nick of time, or Tilly learning to walk.

The movies have not prepared her. Where are Sam, Dean and Bobby when she needs them? Heck, at this point she'd even be happy to see Rufus or tipsy Garth.

"Pleaaaaase!"

The doctor ignores her, instead fussing with his watch a little more.

The nurse leans over, her smile wickedly sharp. "Doctor, two minutes really isn't all that long. Why don't we get started now?"

Bitch.

"Nonsense," says the doctor. It's the first relieving thing to have come out of his mouth since this entire nightmare started. "We must stick to our original plan. Punctuality is a virtue, my dear nurse. By paying attention to time, we can track and solve almost all things. And a gentleman has his word to keep. We wait."

So, there is one asset to these ancient ways. There's little doubt in Tessa's mind that it will do her no good; neither will waiting, but part of her wills those two minutes to pass by so slowly that her heart might stop first.

The nurse gives a grave hum. "I understand how much of a drawing point that is—"

"Shut up already," snaps Tessa. She's barely holding herself together at this point. The tear tracks on her cheeks have only just dried, but she can already feel another wave of them threatening to spill over. "He said no! I still have—I still have time! Christ! You'd think a supposed fellow caregiver would understand the obsession with timeliness."

"Impudent brat," snarls the nurse. "The mouth that you have on you! I have never seen a woman of your stature be so brazen. It's unbefitting of your kind."

Tessa calls her a very unkind word—one that she's more than likely never heard, though perhaps read in adaptations of *Chaucer's Queynte.*

Even the doctor raises his eyebrows. "I dare say, she does have a sharp tongue."

The nurse takes that as her moment to insist. "One that we can rid her of easily, Doctor. Is it truly worth waiting these last two minutes? She is sure to be unclaimed. This one's keeper will not come—neither will she want this one."

The casual racism is washing thin, but Tessa is running out of fight with each tick of the pocket watch.

The allure of being able to do whatever sick tests they've got planned proves to be too much for the doctor. Finally, he turns his attention away from the watch. "Alright," he says. "We shall just begin our preparations now, and on the dot, we shall begin."

"No," begs Tessa. "You don't have to do this! Please, just let me go, just let me go!"

"Mood swings," he tuts. "The distress her poor owners must have been put through."

Ignoring Tessa's pleas for release, the doctor turns and starts gathering his tools with a series of clanks. The rust-laced tray on wheels is pushed against the table.

An equally foul-looking set of torture tools, claiming to be medical, is set on top of the table. One by one, the doctor begins to fetch his instruments from the cupboard behind him. He pivots on the spot, hardly able to twist in the narrow gap.

The doctor takes a great amount of care in lining them up on the tray, tapping the top and the bottom of each one so that they're meticulously lined up with each other.

The nurse is far more impatient. She keeps shooting Tessa these hauntingly gleeful looks, as if she has spent the entire day waiting for this one moment; a surely bloody and gruesome affair about to unravel in the room.

Each clack of rusted metal makes Tessa's heart stutter in her chest. Her eyes grow wider and wider with each passing sound; despair is a yawning pit in her gut, an unending twisting blackness that sours and spills into her veins, her muscles, the very neurons that make up her body. Fear and anger twist inside of Tessa's heart in equal measure.

Each breath seems harder to pull in than the last. The stale air curls in Tessa's lungs, just one more added bit of discomfort.

A circle of metal is slipped over her head and she fights it—only to have the nurse reach out and thrust her jaw up so hard her teeth clash. Tessa flicks her head from side to side as best she can under the squeeze of sharp claws, but there's no budging. The doctor winds in the screws that hold it in place. They don't break the skin, yet she feels suddenly empathetic to pressed flowers being wound tighter and tighter down in their trap.

And then the doctor picks up what can only be described as a nail and a hammer; if there are medical terms for it, she doesn't know them, but unlike the toffee hammer one which was already there, it's *big*.

There's a bolt of terror whipping at her spine when the point of the nail is pressed to her temple.

She's about to be lobotomized . . .

The tears begin to come in earnest. "Please, please don't do this! Just—just get off of me! Please, just stop, just get off of me!"

Of all the ways Tessa could die, this is the last one that she wants to come true. She's seen horror movies. She knows what it looks like to have something split straight through your skull. It's blood, pain, and an eternity wishing you were dead all rolled up into one neat little hammer strike—if it goes as planned.

The doctor and the nurse continue to ignore her. It's as though they can't even hear Tessa's begging. They can, however, hear the crashing of glass bottles that shatter at the end of the hallway. The nurse's head snaps towards the doorway.

She demands, "What was that?"

"I am not certain." The doctor returns the nail to the tray that he'd set up. His mouth curls down into a sharp frown. "But you had better go and address the issue. We shall commence the procedure as soon as you return. It is a shame, but we must make sure that there are no problems with the other patients. They might need your help."

Tessa's voice cuts in, rasping and frenzied. "She isn't a monster and she can decide for herself. She's disabled and I'm black, you have this totally wrong! I know you don't get it, but the values you have—they're just messed up! No one has believed them for hundreds of years. You're dead; you hear me? Dead!"

"Are you threatening me?" the nurse bites.

"No. I'm being literal!" Tessa drags out the last word.

The nurse purses her lips. "Doctor, I am certain that one of the others can check on it. We already have everything set up. And she is unruly. If we wait much longer, then we will surely encounter issues. It truly might be best if we just proceed with things."

"No, it is best if you go. At least that way I know any issues will be taken care of promptly." That brings a smile to her face and he continues. "Do hurry, as I would like to get this procedure underway." He waves a dismissive hand at the nurse. "There's clearly some sort of ruckus happening in the hallway. I at least have faith in the fact that you will be able to get the problem handled with minimal delays."

The nurse heaves a sigh of rancid breath. "Alright. I will be most quick about it. And I will be certain to give whoever has created the mess a . . . thorough . . . scolding." Her blue eyes twinkle.

The doctor, still dismissive, tells her, "see that you do. I am running a hospital for esteemed clients. Not a zoo for the entertainment of children."

And then her kitten heels *click-clack* on the tile as she turns and makes for the door. The nurse pauses, giving Tessa one last look which is as sour as fresh-picked lemon. Clearly, she's not pleased that it's been delayed even longer. Tessa, however, counts this as the one stroke of good luck that she's had since stepping into this haunted hospital.

Whatever has caused the ruckus out there? Tessa's going to count it as her favorite event of the year.

Finally, the nurse pushes the door open and vanishes out into the hallway. The door closes behind her with a heavy *thunk*. The clack of her heels is cut off when it

does. It's a sound that Tessa will never be able to get out of her head; call her a sneaker wearer for life after this whole disaster.

This might not have changed anything long term, but the brief reprieve from ending doom is still appreciated. The fact that there's no longer a nail threatening to split open her temple with a few taps is—well, saying it's a relief is an understatement! Tessa has done some scary stuff over the years, but this takes the cake. The moldy, spoiled, rancid cake with cheap icing and a poison cherry on top.

All she wanted to do was give Tilly a good video and put a smile on her face. Now it seems like they're both one clock hand tick away from meeting an unkind maker.

Still, the insanity is temporarily halted. A small blessing, but a blessing all the same. Tessa lets out a dandelion-soft sigh.

The doctor takes it as disappointment somehow, living in his own twisted world; his prehistoric views, his one-sided vision. He walks over, pressing a hand to Tessa's face. She tries to jerk away, but the straps don't let her go far. It's like he's attempting to offer a morbid sense of comfort, and yet there's a perversion to the touch. Less like she's a scared person, and more like the doctor is attempting to calm a highly-strung dog. Blood is speckled on the floor— somewhere between a crime scene photo and a Jackson Pollock painting.

Tessa has read about what they did to women back then—how professionals "treated" hysteria, and the last thing she wants is those hands on her.

Cold, frost bitten fingers stroke over Tessa's cheek. Her skin goose pimples.

"There, there," says the Doctor. "It shall be alright soon, you have my word."

"Go to Hell," says Tessa. "That's where you should be at right now, anyway!"

The doctor just clicks his tongue at her, and gives her a firm pat on the cheek. "You'll be feeling better soon, not to worry. She is my favorite nurse, you know. Very perfunctory about things. Very kind."

"That's the most ridiculous thing I've heard in here," Tessa bites.

His empty coal-like eyes drift back to the door. "This should take her no time at all."

All Tessa can do is hope that the doctor is wrong.

# CHAPTER 16.

Tilly pulls herself to a point where she can half-crawl when feet appear in the corridor. It's the skinny nurse, looking as sour-faced as ever as she shuts the door—the one to the treatment room. She pauses just outside of the door, her shrewd gaze raking over the hallway, clearly trying to find the source of the noise.

Maybe it was a good thing that the upper floor broke. At least now, Tilly knows exactly what room they've got Tessa in.

"Hey you!" Tilly-Tok practically spits at the nurse. "Over here!"

Her head snaps towards the pile of injured muscles and dirt on the floor. Attention garnered, she speaks, "Did Nurse Lovett not have you put in your room? You are a frightfully problematic creature, Matilda." She walks towards her, eyes as slit-like as a cat's pupils. "And you're disturbing the treatment of another patient . . . In fact," she taps on her lip. "You should come see your miserable associate. After some medicine, of course, then the doctor can deal with you."

Tilly-Tok wants to get in that room. Letting her know might be a terrible idea. None of the people in this hospital are kind, but there's something about this one particular nurse that just seems . . . so much worse. It's

the way she holds herself, the sharp curve of her thin, ghastly lips.

Thinking fast, she tosses her phone at the ghostly apparition, but it bounces off and slides back at her. Tilly can't quite understand these ghosts, how they can be solid and translucent all at once. There are rules to these spirits, she's certain, but Tilly hasn't been able to figure them out yet.

The nurse hisses and comes down to Tilly, perching on her toes with bent knees. She picks up the phone and turns it around with a tilted head. Leering she throws it back at Tilly who catches it and forces it into her pocket with a clink on the syringe.

The nurse takes the blonde by the hand, so gently that it almost feels like she cares—almost.

"What?" Tilly pants. "You want to hold my hand and get a bedside manner now?"

"Hmph. I really do hope that the doctor chooses me to deal your punishment, you little wretch." With her free hand she clasps Tilly's slimy hair and jerks her head up.

"Tsshh!"

"The doctor thinks that you'll be his crowning glory when he cures you. I think you'll be my crowning glory when I beat that resistance out of you once and for all—call me twisted, but I hope it takes a very . . . very . . . long . . . time."

She hauls Tilly along the sopping floor by one arm, leaving smears in her wake.

“You’re going past the door!” Fire burns in Tilly’s shoulder as they slide past Tessa's room. “Where are you taking me?”

“To take your medicine so you will be quiet like a good girl.”

Before she can protest, they’re outside of the pharmacy.

*Knock! Knock! Knock!*

She raps on the door, pushes it open and practically tosses Tilly inside.

The other nurse answers. “That’s where she was. I did not realize you were dealing with her.”

“I was not supposed to. Get out, Lovett! Go deal with your squealer upstairs.” The skinny nurse jerks a hand towards the stairwell, pointing up it with one sharp tipped finger.

The other nurse places her hands on her hips and stares at her cripplingly cruel co-worker. “Matilda is my patient, Muriel.”

The slender nurse steps towards her, inches from her face. “And yet, you lost her. Need I inform the good doctor of your mistake?”

Lovett puffs up her chest. Clearly, the two nurses don't get along. Funny; guess that means some grudges really do stretch out into the afterlife. Then again, these spirits might not be the best example of that.

It's just the distraction Tilly-Tok needs.

With a shunt of her shoulders, she arches her chest forward. The syringe rolls onto the floor with a small chink. She scoops it towards her before the nurse can see it, curling her arm around it and dragging it towards her chest.

"One day, he will see that you learned everything you know from those hysterics and fallen women. Then he'll see his mistake in being manipulated by his natural urges. You're not even a real nurse—just an ill-trained pharmacist's daughter." Lovett says, her face twisted into a grim, unhappy look.

"Do not compare me to them. Now, let me medicate this monster." Muriel jerks her chin towards Tilly.

Lovett hesitates, then deflates. "Quite right. They want to be well." With that, she leaves—but not without thrusting a wheelchair in. "You can put that away. She's your charge."

It's the same one that Tilly had left in the nurse's room.

Tilly is still messing with the syringe. Her folded fingers keep slipping from the plunger. It's jammed. And she hasn't got the strength to unblock it. Her fingers

twang away like elastic bands as a shadow comes over her.

The nurse is there. She looms in front of Tilly, imposing even in her narrow, twisted form. She hooks Tilly under both arms, dangling her like a dead fish and tossing her into the chair the same way. There is nothing even remotely gentle in the way that she handles Tilly. The chair protests with the force in which Tilly's dropped into it.

The syringe hangs with its point between her fingers—luckily, since with the force she was put back in the chair with, it would have injected her had it been the other way around. There's a crunch behind her. It's definitely freed up. Now she just has to work out how to use it.

"I want to know what you're giving me," she demands as she leans forward. The grime in her hair becomes useful, creating a thick curtain of sludge which she can hide the needle behind. It still isn't pressing, though.

Tilly needs more time. The nurse is moving with a pointed, speedy sort of purpose, though. Clearly, dragging this out is of no interest to her.

Tilly gnaws on her lip. If she wrapped both hands around it and pulled it against her stomach, she could probably unjam it. That would mean spearing all of the liquid without the nurse being in range, though; that's if the contents of the syringe are even anything useful. For all she knows, it could be filled with septic orange juice.

But it's the only option that Tilly has. She's tried, and been unable to come up with any other kind of plan. Finding this syringe was a stroke of luck. If it doesn't work . . . Tilly can't think about that. She just has to figure out how to get the plunger moving.

"I will give you whatever medicine I decide, and you should be grateful. That is what your prescription is, starting with a long overdue sedative, I think." Muriel doesn't even glance in Tilly's direction. The nurse is wholly focused on putting together her concoction of meds.

There is a now all too familiar rattling of glass. She's setting something up. It won't take her long, though.

"Come on, come on, come on," Tilly-Tok whispers as she fights with the glass. Her body is lead weight and that's before the realization hit her that there might just be something she can't do alone.

That thought is terrifying. Tilly pulls in a sharp breath, trying to banish it to the far backs of her mind. This isn't the time to be doubting herself. This is the time to figure things out, and make the situation work.

The nurse comes over, bending down with the point of the needle glinting in the last of the daylight. It draws closer, and closer still.

Tilly leans as far away as she possibly can, huddling against the far side of the wheelchair.

"Give me your arm!" The nurse holds one hand out, as if she honestly expects Tilly to just give it over.

She refuses.

The nurse leans forward to snatch her, and that's when Tilly's head flicks up. The syringe is in her mouth, tongue on the back of it and teeth gripping the tube. She throws herself towards the nurse and the needle plunges in. The liquid deploys.

The nurse does not disappear. *Shit!* Tilly had really been hoping that would just make the woman *poof* or—or something!

Tilly pulls back, shrinking even further into the corner than she was before. Her mouth hangs open as the nurse grasps the needle and pulls it out, smashing it as she throws it against the wall. The nurse's face twists up into an untold fury; Tilly has never seen someone look that mad before, as if it's the only emotion left in them.

Tilly yelps, raising her hands over her face.

"You little—" The nurse screeches, looking truly monstrous as she swoops in on Tilly.

Tilly braces for the pain. She's not sure if she should be expecting a slap or to be thrown bodily to the floor, but either way, it has her tucked up as small as she can make herself. Her eyes close tight—for a second, and another, and another.

Nothing happens.

No pain. No grabbing hands. No snarling, or bitten out words.

Finally, she opens an eye; just in time to see the vapid vapours of her captor disappear like smoke. The nurse is gone, vanquished . . . at least for the time being.

Tilly-Tok pants, chest rising and falling—she got her, literally, by the skin of her teeth. Now, it's the doctor's turn.

She may not have a weapon now, but she has information—they're corporeal, and that means they can be hit.

She grabs the wheels, and she's off.

# CHAPTER 17.

The doctor gives a disgruntled look at his pocket watch. "Where is Muriel? I'm afraid we may have to do this without her."

"No," Tessa says before gulping back the ball of adrenaline which is stripping her throat. "You said you would wait!"

"We cannot wait forever, I am afraid." Licking his lips, he picks the nail back up and carefully inserts it into the hoop. Once more there's a sharp prick on her temple. A bit of rust flakes off and sweeps over her skin like a bug.

"I can be different, I'll behave," Tessa begs.

He sighs. "They all say that. Unfortunately, I have no choice. You see, the common man does not understand the nature of what we do here. They do not comprehend what must be done in the name of progress."

"We . . ." Her sentence gives out. What's the point of telling him the world has made progress? He can't see that he's dead, and doesn't seem to be able to see that the very building around them is falling apart.

His arm raises.

"Stop!" The word had been running through Tessa's head, but it isn't her who says it . . .

The brunette raises her head as much as she's able. "Tilly?"

"Get off her," she says, pushing the door open with the clunky, old footplate. She makes her entrance—fierce as Ru Paul on stage. "We are going to leave."

The doctor lowers his hand with the hammer gripped in it. "Leaving?" He places it on the tray.

"You heard me." Tilly puffs up her chest.

Tilly's hands are shaking. In fact, there's a tremor racking through her entire body, fierce as a leaf caught in a winter gale. It's just as much from exhaustion as it is from fear—and yet, Tilly isn't willing to back down. It's taken her too long to get this far.

The doctor's eyes flash black, like stones. Tilly pulls in a deep breath, clears her throat, and then says it again.

"We're leaving."

His lips press together, fingers drumming on the tray. They tap a steady rhythm, then slow.

"Blast. Procedure is procedure," he says.

Tessa's lips part and she blinks faster than her blood drips on the floor.

The doctor opens the small cabinet and extracts a stack of mildew-soaked papers. These, too, he taps and then his bottom lip raises.

“These are release papers.” He shifts away from the women toward the back of the room where the plank-covered curtains sit. “I had hoped that you wouldn’t come for her,” he muses at the wood as if it is a country view. “Our establishment needs willing participants.”

“Get me out of here!” Tessa shouts, thrashing a few times.

“I will . . . if she could just come over here and sign these.” He tosses the papers down above Tessa's head with a waft of moldy air.

Tilly-Tok narrows her eyes—she knows his tactic.

Tessa cranes her head up. “Bring them to her, she can’t possibly get the chair through there.”

“Tessa,” she starts. “He isn’t going to come over here.”

“But then—!”

“If you are well, you may come and collect these papers, and then you may collect your companion. If not, you lack the capacity and capability to make such a decision.”

Tessa curses at him as Tilly nudges the chair as far into the room as much as she can.

“She can’t get through!”

Tilly lifts her chin. "Tessa . . . Of all people, you should know that what you can do, I can do, and what I can do, you can do."

"I wish that were true, and I'm not treating you differently. We all have our limitations—some different to others, but that doesn't mean we're any less. It's not your fault you can't get to him . . . I don't blame you."

The blonde glances her as tears carve over the mahogany of her skin. "I got this."

"This isn't bloody Glee!"

"No, because . . ." She leans forward, putting her elbows by her support worker's thigh. "that was a dream and . . . sadly, this is reality."

". . . What are you doing?"

There is no air in Tilly's lungs to reply as she hauls her torso up onto the table, just as she does to get back in her seat from her footplates.

It's no higher, but with these injuries, it may as well be a solid wall. Gritting her teeth, she flops over Tessa's legs, inching herself forward.

If she falls now, it's going to kill her. The floor is a daunting streak of filth beneath her. One wrong move, and Tilly's going to slip and snap her neck. Just thinking about it is enough to send phantom twinges of pain rushing through her—along with the real ones.

Tilly's watched enough horror movies that it's actually pretty easy to picture it. Her nose smashing against the wood. Her neck jerking. The blood pooling beneath her. Her breath comes in uneven jagged gasps, sharp through her chest, like the dust in the air has turned into shards of glass.

"I can do this," says Tilly, determination thick in her voice. "I just have to go slow . . . take my time . . . and I'll be able to do this. I won't leave you here, Tessa. I promise."

Her gaze lands on the places where Tessa's arm has been split open, still sluggishly spilling red over the curves of dark skin. Tilly's stomach twists. Her mouth is dry, like she's been eating sand.

Her eyes land on Tessa's face instead. She repeats, "I promise."

Even at risk of falling. Tilly's got to try. She's got to.

"My God," Tessa breathes.

Taking a moment, Tilly shimmies her hips onto the surgical table and sits up. Now, she is sat on the edge of it and can inch along. Her legs hang precariously.

"We could so do free running or rock climbing." She half chuckles; the way people do when they just heard their boss make a seriously offensive joke but they need that promotion.

"Please, be careful."

Inch by inch, she shifts along—skirting the precipice, with the floor swirling in front of her until she reaches the tray on wheels.

Keeping her eyes locked with the doctor, she leans forward a shade and moves it out of her way before continuing her shimmy.

He holds out a pen which she takes between the heels of her hands.

It's hard enough to hold the pen properly. It's even more difficult trying to get the damned thing to work. Like everything else in this hospital, the pen is ancient. Tilly uses her teeth to pull the cap off of it and the old, aged plastic snaps between her teeth. She has to spit out both the cap and broken bits of plastic. It scrapes at her tongue.

A new problem faces her then. Pens dry out. That's some sort of office room curse, right? Grab a pen and the nib's gone dry. That's also the case when the pen happens to be ridiculously old. Using palms and mouth, she manages to twist it back around, and into a position that's at least marginally useable. She pulls in a deep breath.

For a lot of people, signing something is easy work. It's a whole different story for Tilly, and the doctor knows it. He's watching her struggle with a sort of sick glee in his eyes, as though he's already decided that she would fail this challenge.

Tilly, viciously, thinks, *I'll show you. You're not going to take Tessa from me that easily.*

It takes a bit of tricky fumbling, but eventually, Tilly is able to press it to the paper. Nothing. Not a single blot of ink is left behind. "It's not working."

Tessa says, "she can't sign it if the pen won't work."

The doctor, smugly, tells her, "it worked fine for me not a moment ago."

Tilly-Tok mutters, "that's because he sees what was . . . Not what *is*."

Tilly takes a deep breath. She holds the pen out and curls her tongue around the nib of it a few times, moistening it. Then she presses it to the paper once more. This time, it leaves behind a smear of spotty, blue-tinted ink.

She smears her X across the sodden pages.

The doctor taps the papers on the side to straighten the edges, just as he meticulously set out his tools.

His lip wrings into a smile. "Sign you name."

Tessa jerks her head up. "She can't write."

“Oh?” he offers as if he didn’t know that already. “Then how can she possibly sign?”

Tilly’s pulse bumps her chest for the uncountable time today. “I made my mark, now let her go.”

“I request only a signature, not a mark.” The doctor says, and Tilly’s whole heart drops straight into her feet, threatening to pull her off the edge.

Writing her name is an entirely different story from trying to scratch out a few crooked lines. Tilly doesn’t have that kind of dexterity in her fingers, that much grip. Even if the pen worked well, she still wouldn’t be able to do it.

This pen barely scratched out the X mark. Pair that with Tilly’s lack of writing ability and . . . she isn’t sure how she can do it.

For just a moment, the disbelief at the request overwhelms her. The grief. How many times has she been put in a spot just like this? How many times had someone tried to ask Tilly to do something, only for her attempts to be futile?

It’s a crushing feeling. A familiar one, mostly given to her by so-called professionals.

Only today, there’s more at stake than just Tilly’s pride or vanity. Today, Tessa’s life is literally resting on whether Tilly can do what’s asked of her. It makes her feel sick and shaky.

The vlogger looks at her folded fingers with the sparkle stolen from her eyes. "But . . ."

"I am a stickler for the rules, my dear," the doctor says. Tilly knows where her sparkle has gone, he's sucked the little stars into the black holes of his eyes.

She is far from giving up, though. Time for Plan B.

# CHAPTER 18.

"Let me offer her a hug before you begin treatment, surely that's alright?" Tilly-Tok says, looking back at Tessa. The other woman's plump lips are quivering, but her eyes fight to hold onto hope—it's obvious by the way Tilly-Tok is talking that she isn't going to leave. Not without a little push anyhow.

"Be brief, these leanings are unhealthy for you both," he says with a pause. "I shall allow it, however, because the movement shall be good for you."

Tessa makes to embrace her friend, yet finds herself stuck. Still, she raises up a little—what slight width she can anyway. The blonde turns on her hind and leans over her, draping herself wholly over Tessa. The press of the tan-streaked skin is enough to let her know just how exhausted Tilly is. Her skin is squashy with bruises that are ripe to flower. It's a feeling Tessa remembers well from the nursing home. Such frailty; paper-thin skin. It isn't something which she ever expected of the young woman. Even through the tan lines, smudged as though she's been sprayed by the world's dirtiest shower, there are yellow buttercups and the early signs of purple tulips.

"Huh?" Tessa croaks at the wetness on her wrist as the blonde let's herself wholly down. It's sticky, almost like lip gloss.

And then it hits—lips. She glances sideways, getting only a back view of the woman's head, but she's worked it out.

More specifically, Tilly has.

It isn't long before there's a tug of teeth. To begin with, not a lot happens, but then—Tessa can move her wrist! Tilly has pulled open the strap with her mouth.

She has to stay in place, though; one hand isn't enough to free her from the doctor's clutches for long. She needs time to undo the others that Tilly can't reach—and that's something they're lacking.

Tessa taps the side of Tilly's cheek, hoping she'll understand. Her wrist rests under the strap, waiting like an octopus letting a crab get closer and closer to its den. She runs her tongue over her lip as Tilly sits up.

Heels click along the hall, and it's enough to take the doctor's eye for just a second.

"Doctor!" The ghastly nurse is back, blue eyes red with veins and swaying at the door. The moment she sees Tilly, she growls.

"I thought I'd gotten rid of you!" The vlogger gasps.

"Vile and vicious creature!"

Tessa's breath hitches in her chest! Tilly-Tok throws herself at the cart with a clatter, riding it to smash into the wretched nurse. Without thinking, Tessa whips her

arm free to grab her—too late. It thunders, bashing into the wheelchair like a domino. It strikes the nurse and she evaporates in a puff of smoke.

"Tilly!" Tessa grabs her other restraint as the girl hangs over the trolley, clinging with her elbows and slipping by the second. Her legs aren't going to hold her. Little as she is, her weight dropping could snap her ankles in a second. She slides, yet somehow manages to stay on.

But the doctor has seen Tessa now.

He lurches towards her and grabs her newly freed wrists.

Tessa works hard to try and free herself, twisting in the grip of the doctor. She's so close to freedom that she can practically taste it, and so close to getting to Tilly . . . but the doctor is inhumanly strong. Tessa's ankles are still bound. No matter how much she flails, she can't seem to toss the man off of her.

"I don't know how you slipped that . . . But . . . You will not . . . be getting any bedside manner . . . now."

"Hurry!" Tilly squeals.

The doctor is so strong, though. His grip slices against her sore wrists like barbed wire. He manages to pin one down, quickly trying to strap it in. This leaves her other arm free, however, and Tessa takes full advantage of that fact. She slaps the man with all of her strength. The sound of skin hitting skin fills the room.

There's a half-second where the force of Tessa's blow has led him to turn away from her. When the doctor turns back to face her once again, there is pure fury in his blackened gaze.

Moving fast like only someone with a lot of practice in the action can do, the doctor unhooks his belt, pulls it from the loops of his slacks, and strikes Tessa with it. Large welts form in the wake of the hit. The snap of leather is all-consuming. Pain makes stars burst to life in Tessa's vision. She shouts unbidden, nearly biting her tongue when she does. The pain makes tears flow down her cheek.

Tessa struggles to remember how to breathe. The room is so small and so dark. It's crowded and sour in the way that only old things are; they could so very easily die in this building and never be found, left to join the rot and the decay that is already clinging to the building. Two more ghosts in a sea of endless death. Two more stars that fade out beneath the blackness of night.

If they don't make it out of here—and fast—then . . . no. Tessa refuses to think about that. Not now. Not ever.

Her breath hiccups in her chest. The doctor makes another attempt to pin Tessa's hand back into the strap. Tilly makes a frightened sound, slipping even further forward. Pain and darkness or not, Tessa refuses to just give up. Tilly has already done so much to get here—now it's Tessa's turn to fight through her fears and finish getting them out.

They're so close to freedom. Giving up now is out of the question. Even with the threat of getting belted again, Tessa understands that she has to act. She shakes her head, trying to clear the stars from her vision. As Tessa does so, her gaze lands on the machine above her.

Like everything in the Doctor's surgery, it's a relic of another time. There's no way it should work—but there's also no way that the ghosts should be here, no way that the mixture in that nurse's syringe should have really knocked Tessa out. They're riding the line between existence and fraud.

Tessa hopes that for once in this awful day, that line will bend in her favor.

"You know," Tessa says. "The way you treat people, it's just not cool. In fact, it's shocking!" She reaches up with her free hand and grasps a metal rod—the arm of the long since powered down electric shock machine.

"Strike me and strike yourself!" He clutches her.

"Pleeaaase." Tilly is sinking and something rolls off the tray as her knees begin to bend and her elbows struggle to hold her.

"Maybe in your time, but hopefully, not mine!" Tessa jabs him and, true to his word, his body starts to jolt . . . and so does hers—fortunately only because he is holding her, though.

There's no true power in the building anymore, and nothing that can course through Tessa's veins. The doctor, however, has never moved on. He's stuck in the past, with the power, the medicine. Bright bursts of light dance over his skin, sparks of static electricity that zap and hum in the air.

He shouts but the sound is garbled. The doctor's pitch-black eyes roll back into his head. He spasms so hard that his grip on Tessa's shirt makes her bounce along with him. The dead machine hums as if it's really turned on.

Sparks fly—literally. The rod feels like it's shaking in Tessa's grip. She clings to it even tighter, refusing to pull it away from the doctor just yet. He must try to say something, but there's no way to get it out. His grip on her finally goes lax.

The moment he falls back and disappears, she sits up, hauling her wrist away. The belt snaps.

"Now you break!" she shouts, slipping her hands under Tilly's armpits as she drops, just in time.

Tessa pulls her onto the surgical table with zero grace. She yanks the metal ring from her head with a scratch and tosses it away.

"Be quick," Tilly-Tok pants, leaning over to rip open an ankle strap with her teeth. "He'll be back."

Tessa rips the other open. "How do you know?"

"Already took the nurse out once. Come on!" It frees.

The support worker swings her legs over the bench, landing her boots with a splash. Water is coming in. There's another crash along the corridor.

"This place is caving in. Time to go. Ready?" She snatches Tilly up without an answer.

"I thought you'd never ask!"

With her arms wrapped tightly around the blonde, the brunette dashes out along the falling corridor. Her feet splash and she slides as a nurse comes from the secret hatch.

"Run!" Tilly gasps, holding on for dear life.

"I'm trying! There's another nurse!"

A wall falls in.

A woman with matted black hair and bruises covering her arms and face – the clear welt-covered strips of a belt that had struck her – grabs the nurse from behind. She snarls and pulls the nurse back up the passageway with broken sounds.

The nurse fights in the woman's grip, but enough has been changed to allow her to hold on. Her eyes flash black and glassy. The nurse vanishes from sight, but her howling screams echo along the corridor, but neither woman stops to see what dreadful fate has befallen the nurse.

They go as fast as Tessa can, down the stairs and out of the door. She spins and bashes through with her back, not stopping.

At the end of the crumbling corridor are black eyes.

The grass is still a welcome relief beneath their feet. It cleans the filth from the soles of Tessa's shoes. The nurse follows them outside; they can leave the building. The new question is: how far can they go?

It's not something that Tessa wants to figure out. Her entire body feels as if it's been lit on fire. Running and carrying Tilly has ripped the wounds on her arms back open, leaving ruddy red stains against the mess that is already Tilly's clothing. Each rub of fabric against the split open skin just makes it burn that much worse.

The nurse lets out an inhuman, wordless scream behind them. Then sounds, garbled, as if coming through a radio thick with static. "Get back here, you wretch!"

Tessa doesn't stop. She refuses to so much as give the nurse the satisfaction of a backward glance.

"Hurry," Tilly shouts. With the angle that she's being held, Tilly has no choice but to look back at the nurse. "She's gaining on us!"

Tessa is panting too hard to really answer. Her lungs are igniting. The air scrapes her throat raw, like a mouthful of sand paper. But she's almost there! The chain is just up the way!

Tessa hits the dirt path. Her footsteps are thundering beneath her. She grips Tilly so tight that it's likely to leave even more bruises on the other woman's skin. Though, really, bruises are the least of their worries right then.

Finally, the chain is in view!

"Almost there," she pants out. The words make her throat feel even worse. She's struck with the realization that she's hungry, and so thirsty it's making her split-open lips cling to the fronts of her teeth.

Tessa jumps the chain, closely followed by the nurse. She glances back just in time to see the building fold in on itself and the ghost disappear.

"She's gone," says Tilly.

"I'm not stopping."

"Definitely not asking you to."

By the time they reach the adapted vehicle, Tessa's arms are lead.

She pulls the passenger-side door open, gripping Tilly with one arm. She places her on the seat and slams the door, running around and leaping in.

"Think you can manage your own belt with all that newfound independence?" Tessa turns the key and stamps on the accelerator pedal.

“Yeah, just get us away from here.” She pulls it up and around with the heel of her hands. There’s a click of metal on metal.

Tessa glances the mirror. “Nothing following.”

“Thank God.”

As the wheels hit tarmac, every ounce of Tessa relaxes. The muscles in her arms go slack, her shoulders slumping down. For what seems like the first time since the nurse first appeared, Tilly’s heart beats at a normal pace. They’ve done it. They survived. Her head slumps back on the seat.

“Smart trick with your teeth.”

“Learned it in hydrotherapy—don’t ask.”

“Wasn’t going to. Sorry about leaving your chair.”

“Better than leaving me. Nice work with the electricals, by the way.”

Tessa thanks her, and they don’t speak again for five miles.

“Bloody Hell. What a trip,” Tessa says.

“You’re telling me.”

“All we need now is to see that Jeepers Creepers van.”

Tilly’s eyes bore into her as hard as the nail nearly did. “Don’t even joke about that.”

# CHAPTER 19.

Once they get home, three things are in order; coffee, pain killers and a wash.

"I'll go run you a bath."

"No!" The word is out of Tilly's mouth before her brain has even had chance to process it. She pats her pinafore dress down. It's caked in . . . God only knows what, and the white of her top is the same color as hundred-year-old photographs. "I don't know if I can handle getting in one more tub today, even if it's pristine porcelain. A shower would be great, though."

"A shower it is, then."

"I can't wait to wash the stink of that place off me."

"I thought you said it was pristine."

Tilly-Tok tuts. "Their opinions were dirt."

"I hail that like Whoopi Goldberg singing gospel in a nunnery."

They make it into the bathroom, and Tessa helps Tilly get set down on the shower chair. It feels harder than usual on her bottom. All of the bad landings that she took today really left her bruised and aching.

First, the water is set to run and warm up. Then it's turned to come out through the shower head. The warm water splatters against Tilly. It's like the best sort of balm; cleaning away the slime, the muck, and the grime. Soothing away the aches of her muscles and her skin.

Tilly can't help but sigh into it as she's washed off. Inch by inch, the dark brown filth is pushed from Tilly's skin. Inch by inch, she starts to feel alive again.

Once all the filth is dread off of her, Tessa grabs a nice fluffy towel and goes to help with Tilly's hair.

"I've got it," says Tilly. She grabs the towel between her palms and starts trying to dry off her hair. The towel is soft and damp beneath her palms. It's a struggle, but there's a wave of relief when she's able to do it by herself. It's maybe not as totally dry as it could be, but it's dry enough not to soak her pillow case later.

Tessa gives her a grin, pride shining in her eyes. Count that as a step in the right direction. The only step forward that Tilly is going to be taking today, but still. A step in the right direction is still a step, even if it's a tiny one.

The brunette's hands reach for the moisturizer and offers it out. "Are you doing this?"

"One thing at a time."

"Fair play." She unscrews the cap and rubs it in with a circular motion. "As much as I love this newfound independence, I'm carrying you to bed."

Tilly lifts her yellowing arms. "With these, I'm not going to argue!"

"Just this once, though." Tessa finishes putting the moisturizer onto Tilly's skin and twists the top back on. "Once those bruises are gone, no being lazy."

"Only on weekends."

Tilly may be covered in bruises, but pulling the quilt up over herself in bed is a feeling of pure bliss.

Tessa asks, "I hate to put a dampener on this, but what are you going to do without the wheelchair?"

"I can manage without it for a couple of days if you stay."

Tessa laughs as Tilly orders one on her phone and tosses it on the side. "Of course, I'm staying, besides, I am not driving home in the dark after that!

They both settle into the bed together, under the sheets, taking a moment to just completely enjoy the comfort of the soft mattress, the warm quilt, and the pillows beneath their heads. It might be an even better feeling than getting a shower!

Having something soft and giving beneath her is a blessing. She's sure that Tessa feels the same way about laying on a bed, after having been strapped into that awful table for so long.

The fact that Tilly's not alone just yet after that ordeal is a really helpful thought, too. Tilly's not scared of the

dark, but she shares the same views as Tessa right then: she doesn't want to be alone in the dark tonight. It seems to smother them. Tilly faintly regrets not leaving one of the lights on, but she's sure not going to ask Tessa to get out of bed for something like that.

Neither of them have any plans of getting back up until the sun is high, high in the sky above them.

Silence blankets them, but it's quickly broken by Tessa saying, "I'm sorry we couldn't get any footage while we were out today."

"Me too," says Tilly. And then, "I think my next video is just going to be me telling a ghost story."

"That would work," says Tessa. "You've sure got the inspiration for it. Just do me a favor and leave me out of the cast."

A smile splits over Tilly's face. She can't help herself, tacking on, "or I might find a haunted hotel to stay in. That seems like a pretty great idea too! It could be a series. Tilly-Tok goes to Haunted Local."

"Tilly-Tok."

"Yeah?"

"Piss off."

They laugh until they fall asleep—not that it takes very long after that day.

Peridot.

Printed in Great Britain
by Amazon

64103828R00102